The Pickleball Girl Finds Her Match

WHISPER HILLS COUNTRY CLUB — **Book 1**

The Pickleball Girl Finds Her Match

REBECCA JASMINE

GREENLEAF
BOOK GROUP PRESS

This book is a work of fiction. Names, characters, businesses, organizations, places, events, and incidents are either a product of the author's imagination or are used fictitiously. Any resemblance to actual persons, living or dead, events, or locales is entirely coincidental.

Published by Greenleaf Book Group Press
Austin, Texas
www.gbgpress.com

Copyright © 2025 Rebecca Jasmine

All rights reserved.

Thank you for purchasing an authorized edition of this book and for complying with copyright law. No part of this book may be reproduced, stored in a retrieval system, or transmitted by any means, electronic, mechanical, photocopying, recording, or otherwise, without written permission from the copyright holder.

Distributed by Greenleaf Book Group

For ordering information or special discounts for bulk purchases, please contact Greenleaf Book Group at PO Box 91869, Austin, TX 78709, 512.891.6100.

Design and composition by Greenleaf Book Group
Cover design by Greenleaf Book Group
Cover images used under license from ©Adobe Stock/Ranta Images; ©Adobe Stock/yaron; ©Adobe Stock/D Graphics

Publisher's Cataloging-in-Publication data is available.

Print ISBN: 979-8-88645-334-8

eBook ISBN: 979-8-88645-335-5

To offset the number of trees consumed in the printing of our books, Greenleaf donates a portion of the proceeds from each printing to the Arbor Day Foundation. Greenleaf Book Group has replaced over 50,000 trees since 2007.

Printed in the United States of America on acid-free paper

25 26 27 28 29 30 31 32   10 9 8 7 6 5 4 3 2 1

First Edition

For Jeremy,
*the best partner this pickleball girl
could ever dream of.*

"Rip, Bang, Win, Cake!"

—Anna Leigh Waters,
professional pickleball player

Pickleball Girl
REFERENCE GUIDE

WHAT IS PICKLEBALL?

Pickleball is a paddle sport that combines elements of tennis, ping-pong, and badminton but differs in that it has a non-volley zone that is called the kitchen. Players may not hit the ball while standing in the kitchen unless the ball has already bounced on their side.

 **2–4 PLAYERS**

 **INDOOR OR OUTDOOR**

The ball is struck back and forth across the net until a player fails to return the ball. Points are scored only by the serving side when the server or the server's team wins the rally, or the opposing side commits a fault.

EQUIPMENT

PADDLES ARE SOLID & LARGER THAN PING-PONG PADDLES, & SMALLER THAN TENNIS RACQUETS

A PICKLEBALL IS SIMILAR TO A WIFFLE BALL, MADE OF PLASTIC WITH HOLES IN IT

NETS ARE SIMILAR TO TENNIS NETS

HOW TO PLAY

THE FIRST SERVE MUST BE MADE DIAGONALLY FROM **A** TO **C**. THE SERVER MUST ALTERNATE SERVES BETWEEN SIDES **A** AND **B**.

The receiver can return the serve anywhere on the server's court in an effort to make the server fault, in which case the receiver will become the server. If the receiver faults first, the server gets a point and changes sides for the next serve. Only the server can score points.

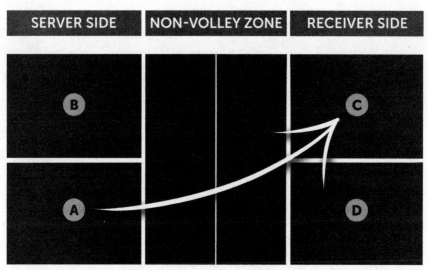

THE GOAL OF THE GAME IS TO WIN BY SCORING MORE POINTS THAN YOUR OPPONENT.

SCORING

Matches are played in a best-of-three format. The first person or team to reach 11 points and leading by at least a 2-point margin wins.

In doubles pickleball, the score is made up of three numbers (for instance, 0-0-2). The first number is the serving team's score. The second number is the receiving team's score. The third number is the server number, which is either server #1 or server #2.

Sources: USA Pickleball, usapickleball.org

Prologue
Whisper Hills Country Club

Midnight

It stank. Even from all the way across the street, she could smell the harsh chemicals. A burned rubber odor carried over on the desert breeze. Draining the last sip of Rombauer from her wine glass, she quietly opened the metal gate from her patio and signaled to the dog. He got up from the warm pavers while she secured a leash to his leather collar, as HOA rules dictated.

Across the street, four brand-new pickleball courts, converted from a single tennis court, glowed in the moonlight. Thick white stripes contrasted with the freshly painted dark-green and royal-blue surface.

Buttoning her cardigan against the evening chill, she dropped the dog's leash. Sensing freedom, he sniffed the grass border, then found his way across the painted asphalt. Tucking his back legs and squatting, the dog dropped a pile of feces atop the newly laid surface of the pickleball courts.

"Ah . . ." Her lips lifted in a cold smile. "Who's a good boy?"

1

"Step away, please," said the emergency medical tech as he moved toward the man on the ground. "Give him some air."

The Palm Springs Medical Response emergency van idled curbside, its red lights flashing round and round. Moments before, music had blared from a wireless speaker on a table under a nearby shade awning, and shouts and laughter had filled the air. But all had quieted when the ambulance pulled up.

"I'm fine," wheezed Paul Rothman, a sheen of sweat above his unruly eyebrows. "I'm fine!" He lay on his back, splayed on the warm green surface, his T-shirt clinging to his soft belly.

The EMT placed his medical bag on the ground and knelt down next to Paul. He rubbed his trimmed salt-and-pepper beard as the walkie-talkie on his chest squawked.

"Third injury on a court today," he said, "and it's not even lunchtime yet."

The EMT's younger partner peered over his aviator sunglasses and looked across the twenty Whisper Hills Country

Club pickleball courts. The players, mostly senior citizens, many with one or two knee braces or an elbow sheathed in a compression wrap, stood or leaned against the low chain-link fence, watching.

He nodded, then answered with his voice low, "We weren't half as busy before pickleball decided to become the fastest-growing sport in the galaxy."

"You aren't old enough to remember how bad it was when rollerblading came on the scene. Now *that* was busy," the older EMT chuckled.

A metallic clank rang out as Endy Andrews threw open the gate and rushed onto the pickleball court. She looked around, her eyes wide and her long, dark hair wild from her mad dash to where Paul lay. She crouched down beside the heavyset man.

"Paul, are you okay?" she asked, her voice breaking. "What happened?"

The bearded EMT held out his hand. "Miss, you're going to need to stand back." He reached out to grab Endy's arm.

"It's okay. I work here," replied Endy. "And Paul is my friend."

"Oh, Endy, I'm fine. I just got a little dizzy," said Paul. He looked at Endy and made a motion to push his gray-blond hair off his sweaty forehead. Endy tucked her own flyaway hair behind her ears, her eyes questioning.

From the corner of his mouth, Paul whispered, "That one's hot. And he's not wearing a wedding ring."

Endy glanced at the younger EMT as he pulled a blood pressure cuff from his kit, a small grin playing on his lips.

Endy's cheeks colored and she stammered, "Oh my god, Paul."

Paul turned his head to the EMT. "An emergency medical technician is a noble profession. Tell me, did you go to an Ivy League college and are you wealthy?"

The EMT's eyebrows drew together over his sunglasses. "Umm, no," he answered.

"I ask because she's been alone for a couple of years, ever since she was jilted by her rich, debonair ex-boyfriend," said Paul, shifting his eyes in Endy's direction.

Endy glanced down at her left hand, where she no longer wore an engagement ring. She slipped her hand under her leg.

"Paul, you don't have to keep telling every handsome guy under the age of forty that Bennett broke up with me," Endy said. "And he wasn't *that* rich."

Paul waved his hand and then placed it on Endy's knee. "We're all looking after your best interests, sweetheart. We don't like seeing how lonely you are."

Out of habit, Endy's left thumb caressed her empty ring finger. "I'm not lonely," she insisted.

"Don't worry about it," the EMT replied, amused. He wrapped the blood pressure cuff around Paul's arm. "But actually, I have a girlfriend. We're getting married this summer, next to a lake in Tahoe."

"Hmm, that's too bad for us," Paul sighed. "The girlfriend part, not the lake part. I love Tahoe in the summer."

It was as if the EMT had placed the blood pressure cuff around her heart and pumped it tight. Endy took a deep breath to try and halt the clenching feeling in her chest. The thought of any summer wedding in Tahoe still wrecked her.

Because *she* should have been the one getting married in Tahoe.

Instead, the band was canceled, invitations withdrawn, and her two-carat diamond engagement ring returned.

When Bennett had broken up with Endy to get back together with his ex-girlfriend, Endy had been floored. They had had a long engagement and were just months from the wedding. But he'd left her. Bennett had just simply left.

And Endy, her heart broken in a million pieces, had ended up alone.

Ever since the breakup, Endy questioned whether it was even possible for her to find someone again. She didn't want anything special . . . just someone she couldn't stop staring at, someone who made her laugh, someone whose arms would wrap around her in a perfect fit. And most importantly, someone with whom she could be herself—unadorned, unchanged, unapologetic.

A relationship completely unlike the one she had had with Bennett.

But, two years later, Endy had not met anyone she was interested in enough to go on more than a couple of dates with. The fact was, she worked and lived in a city that didn't offer a lot of options. The men, with their median age of sixty, gray hair—if any at all—and dinner times beginning at five o'clock, were more like her grandfather than potential suitors. How was she supposed to meet someone, let alone fall in love again?

Maybe Paul wasn't so wrong . . . Endy probably was a little lonely.

A flock of geese honked their way overhead, casting shadows across the pickleball court, and Endy raised her hand to shade her eyes. She watched the geese disappear behind a stand of tall palm trees.

"So, tell me what happened before we got here," said the hot EMT, moving his finger back and forth in front of Paul's eyes.

Paul sighed. "I was playing pretty aggressively for a bit, and set up to hit a dink into the kitchen, but then I got a little nauseous and went to sit down under the awning. I didn't make it far before I got dizzy and had to—"

"Did you just say 'a dink into the kitchen'?" asked the baffled EMT, his head cocked.

"It's a drop shot into the non-volley zone," huffed Paul. "Everybody knows tha—"

"He fell to his knees," interrupted a short, wiry man as he approached, his hand still clutching a pickleball paddle. "His symptoms presented what could have been heatstroke or even a heart attack. Neither is anything to mess around with."

"I told him that I was just dehydrated," said Paul. "But Steven is a retired doctor. He insisted on calling 911."

Endy got up from the court. "Paul tends to overdo—"

"No, I don't," interrupted Paul.

"Yes, you do," replied Endy. "Just last week you had those headaches from actually being dehydrated."

The EMT removed the blood pressure cuff and held out his hand to help Paul sit up. "Well, you both are probably right. While your vitals seem fine now, the nausea and dizziness are concerning." He tucked his equipment into his kit. "Go home and take a cool shower, drink a lot of fluids, and make an appointment to see your doctor as soon as you can . . . just to be on the safe side." His mirrored sunglasses reflected the red lights still flashing at the curb.

"Thank you for getting here so quickly," Paul said, nodding. He leaned into the EMT and added in a conspiring way, "But are you sure you don't want to, maybe, take Endy out for dinner and get to know her?"

"I would if I weren't already taken." The EMT's lips pulled up on the side. "She might actually be hotter than the desert in summer."

"And she's more than mortified with this whole interaction," interrupted Endy, rolling her eyes and placing her hand on Paul's shoulder. "Thanks, guys. We'll take care of Mr. Matchmaker from here."

Endy walked with the EMTs as they carried their equipment back to their van. Once in the cab, the older EMT leaned out his open window.

"You seem like a catch, so I'm sure you'll find someone somewhere." His hand gestured out past Endy. "With the massive interest in this sport, who knows, maybe you'll meet your soulmate through pickleball."

The EMT knocked his fist on the door, then turned off the flashing red lights, and the van started pulling away from the curb.

Endy raised her hand in a wave and looked out over the courts filled with retirees. She shouted after the retreating EMTs, "Sure, and maybe it'll snow in August in Palm Springs!"

She heard a burst of laughter from their open windows, followed by a lively *brruuup, brruuup* of the siren.

Endy turned back to the pickleball courts when high-pitched yapping filled the air. A slender, speckled bird with a crest on its head streaked past, its long legs propelling it swiftly across the grass lawn. Steps behind, a ten-pound miniature dachshund took chase, a flash of angry red-brown fur, floppy ears, and bared teeth.

"Rusty!" shouted Gary Lombardi. He ran after the dog, an empty leash dragging behind him. "Come back here, you beast!"

The roadrunner darted under a bougainvillea and the mini-dachshund followed, skidding under the bush just as the roadrunner squeezed through the wrought iron fencing, making a Houdini-like escape.

Endy and Gary rushed to where a vexed Rusty was holed up, still yapping, biting, and tearing at the vegetation in front of the fence. Endy dropped to her knees and reached out to grab the dog.

"Woah, woah! Don't do that unless you want to get your hand bit off," Gary warned. "We'll have to wait until she tires herself out or—"

"I can get her out of there."

Endy turned toward the voice and craned her head up to find the most gorgeous guy she'd ever seen towering above her.

He nudged past Endy and knelt down, pulling branches aside. "Ouch!" he hissed and yanked his hand back from a spine hidden among the bougainvillea's papery flowers. A bright red scratch bloomed on his skin, and he wiped his hand across the front of his tennis shorts, leaving a smear of blood. From below the bush, Rusty yapped incessantly, but then snarled, low and menacing, and sprang forward, snapping her teeth.

The gorgeous guy moved back, bumping into Endy. Their eyes met and held.

Endy's heart thudded as she got to her feet. Her palms grew damp, and she wiped them on her skirt, at the same time trying to settle the fluttering feeling in her chest.

"Uh . . . hi," she stammered and gave him a slight, oddly formal nod.

He lifted an eyebrow and flashed her a crooked smile, and Endy felt a flush rise in her cheeks.

"Hi," he replied and then grabbed the hem of his T-shirt with both hands crossed in front of him and pulled the shirt up over his head, revealing his rock-hard six-pack abs and chiseled chest.

Endy's jaw dropped open. *Holy crap.* The hot EMT had nothing on this guy.

He wrapped the shirt fabric around his hands and forearms and leaned back into the bougainvillea.

"Careful," groaned Gary, peaking through his hands covering his face. "I can't be held liable for what may happen—"

The mini-dachshund snarled again and her razor-sharp teeth chomped out as the gorgeous guy reached deep under the shrub.

And then, surprisingly, he stood up, the red-brown ball of rage wrapped in his T-shirt, now perfectly quiet. He smoothed the fabric away from Rusty's head and raised her up to examine.

Gary tripped back in terror. "Not so near your face!"

But the tiny dog peeked her nose out, sniffed at the guy's cheek, and then enthusiastically began licking his mouth and chin. He tilted his head back and laughed, the sound deep and full.

"Hey, Hall! I'll meet you on court nine," came a shout from across the lawn, near the tennis courts.

He waved his hand over his head in acknowledgment, then picked up the leash that Gary had dropped on the lawn, clipped it to the dog's collar, and placed her gently on the ground. Rusty hopped up and down on her back legs, trying to climb his leg, but he handed the leash to Gary and then reached down and caressed the dog's soft ears.

And as Endy stood paralyzed, he shook out his T-shirt, pulled it back over his head, and took a step away. He paused and turned to look back at Endy. His lips pulled up in a sexy smile, and then he gave her the same slight, oddly formal nod she'd given him and jogged off.

Gary picked up Rusty and settled her in the crook of his arm. "Endy," he said, "you can close your mouth now." Grinning like a Cheshire cat, he reached out his hand and lifted her chin.

Endy drew in a deep breath and quickly blinked her eyes. Did that really just happen? Did the universe just drop the most gorgeous guy in front of her after she'd declared the chances of meeting someone less than zero? She shook her head, wondering if her morning could get any stranger, and looked across the lawn to the pickleball court where she had just been with the EMTs. Paul Rothman waved in her direction.

"Drama over," Paul called out. "I'm giving it up for the day, so everyone, please, resume playing."

The rest of the pickleball players slowly moved from where they sat. Some raised their paddles in acknowledgment, a couple waved, and they all returned to their courts. The music was turned back on, and the squeaking of shoes moving on the court resumed.

Paul turned to Steven and the two other men who had been on the court with them but had stood to the side during the ordeal. "You guys should keep playing."

"I don't know, Paul, that just doesn't seem right," argued Steven.

"I'm *fine*, Steven. I'll be at home resting and drinking this." Paul held up a large bottle of fruit punch Gatorade.

Steven looked reluctant. "Well, we don't even have a foursome."

Returning to the group, Endy raised her hand. "I'll play in."

Paul nodded. "See, Endy will join you. Seriously, you all keep playing."

"As long as you're sure . . ." Endy pulled out her phone from her pocket to check the time, then turned to the other men. "But I can only play for a little while—I have a meeting I'll need to get to."

"Okay then, let's play as long as we can," replied Steven. He turned to Paul. "I'll check in with you this afternoon, okay?"

"That's very nice of you, Steven. I'll see you later." He lifted his Gatorade in a toast. "Have a good match."

Steven tossed Endy the plastic ball as she moved to the baseline. She took a deep breath, refocusing her thoughts. After a beat, she called out the beginning score, "Zero, zero," and, per pickleball rules, added that she was the second server who started the match, "two."

Endy looked across the court, then dropped the ball, swung her paddle, and served the ball over the net.

The foursome played for an hour, with the scores fairly even throughout. Endy didn't even need to pull back on her own play to allow the older men an advantage, although, at age twenty-eight, she often found herself the youngest player on the Whisper Hills courts.

That was the thing about pickleball: anyone could get proficient pretty quickly. And regardless of age, experience, or ability, everyone agreed that playing pickleball was more than just plain fun—it was a way of life.

After their match concluded, Endy stood beneath the shade awning with a dozen other players, drinking from their colorful stainless steel water bottles, chatting and laughing. Every few minutes, golf carts or e-bikes cruised past the area, with people leaning out and waving their hellos. A resounding cheer came from a nearby court, and two of the players high-fived and touched their paddles together.

"Endy, I want to apologize for Paul's behavior with those EMTs," said Steven. "Your love life is none of our business, even if we all think of you like a daughter."

"Thank you, Steven," said Endy. "But everyone here, including Paul, has been wonderful to me. Besides, I don't actually have a love life."

"Well, when you eventually meet some young man who adores you as much as we all do, don't let him Bennett you."

"I'll try my best not to get Bennetted again," said Endy, giving a dry laugh. "Don't worry, if I fall in love with a guy who has a beautiful, sophisticated ex-girlfriend, I'll call it quits with him before he can call it quits with me."

"Cut him off with surgical precision."

"Will do, Dr. Markowitz," Endy assured him with a smile. "I need to get going. Would you text me later and let me know how Paul is doing?"

Steven sat down in the shade of the awning. "Of course, Endy. Don't worry. I'm sure he'll be fine. We've seen worse, right?"

As if on cue, a woman on the next court over shuffled back, trying to reach a ball soaring over her head, then tumbled backward to the hard ground. She caught herself partially on an outstretched hand, but her face grazed the court's surface. Blood bloomed on her cheek as the other three players rushed to her aid. "I'm okay," the woman called out. "I'm okay."

"Go get to your meeting . . . I've got this," Steven said as he slid a glance to Endy and headed for the injured woman. "It's just another regular day of pickleball."

Endy shrugged, palms turned up. "I'll have some ice sent over from the pro shop," she called out over her shoulder, then said under her breath, "Please, let's get through the day without having to call another ambulance."

Country music blared from the wireless speaker and two small white dogs yapped as they wrestled on the freshly mowed grass, turning their fur a brilliant lime green. The thwack of paddles hitting hard plastic balls echoed throughout the surroundings as Endy stepped out of the awning's shade and into the golden California sun shining across the rows and rows of crowded pickleball courts.

2

Endy jogged toward the country club's racquet pro shop. She checked the time on her phone and saw that she would have about forty-five minutes to get her thoughts in order before the community meeting started. The bright desert sun beat down on her dark brown hair, glinting off the natural highlights, and she reached up and pulled it into a high ponytail. A bead of sweat trailed down her long neck, and her upper lip glistened.

Yanking open the glass door to the pro shop, she was hit with a wall of air-conditioning and the ringing of a telephone. "It's going to be super hot today," Endy said, walking inside and fanning her face.

"It's always super hot here," replied Maria Gutierrez as she hung socks on wall pegs. "It's so hot even my ex's heart is melting." Ignoring the ringing telephone, she looked over her shoulder to Endy. "Did you hear the latest?"

"No. What happened?" asked Endy, her eyebrows drawn together.

"The court maintenance crew found more dog crap on the new pickleball courts this morning," replied Joel from behind the front desk as he reached for the telephone. "Second time this week... We don't really know what's going on." He stared at the telephone, which had ceased ringing.

Maria pretended to retch. "I'm sure there's a good explanation," she said. "Joel, I would suppose as the director of racquet sports that you'd know everything that's going on."

"Well, not *everything*," said Joel. "I don't know who's allowing their dog to crap on the courts, but it's disgusting."

"Remember when someone kept leaving their bagel and cream cheese by the patio workout area?" asked Endy. "And no one found it until it started smelling and was covered in all those ants?"

"It turned out to be Mrs. Davis. She thought she'd finish the bagel after her workout, but always forgot about it," Maria said.

"I mean, she *was* eighty-seven."

Maria nodded, agreeing with Endy. "And then there was that time that someone kept collecting all the lemons that dropped from the fruit trees and kept them in that cardboard box by the ice machine, and the whole thing turned into a fermented mush," said Maria.

"Maria," replied Endy. "That was you."

Maria looked chastened. "I was going to make preserved lemons to sell at the farmers' market."

"Again, disgusting," said Joel.

"Maybe it's like an old dog that has trouble going poo, and it can only do it in a specific spot. My *tia* had a little Chihuahua that had to turn around three times and face north before it would actually go."

Hearing this, Endy stopped and slowly cocked her eyebrow at Maria.

Maria shrugged her shoulders. "Or maybe that was my *tio* who had to do that—I can't really remember. I'll call her later and ask."

The door to the pro shop opened, and in came a few groups of players that had just come off their courts. Club members called out to one another, gathering around the café tables, and the volume in the pro shop rose. The deafening whir of a smoothie blender competed with the TVs mounted high above the counters, combined with a heated debate over the benefits of hat versus visor.

Endy stood in front of the wall of windows with a smile, the radiant sunlight warming her back.

"Just get one of both," she called out to the women contemplating the hat display. "Members get twenty percent off merch."

Behind the desk, Maria nodded at Endy and tapped her temple. *Smart*, she mouthed over the loud music playing from the wall speakers, while the women approached the desk carrying two hats and two visors.

Endy moved away from the windows and weaved between the half dozen tables sprinkled throughout the pro shop café, stopping next to a group of older, gray-haired men, their pickleball paddles piled on the table. One had a look of concentration across his face as he sucked at his teeth with his tongue.

"Why do they call these smoothies when they're anything but? They should be called crunchy drinks," said George Jacobs. He pulled his lips open and bared his teeth. "Do I have anything in my teeth?"

Endy choked back a laugh when she saw the bunches of tiny chia seeds sprinkled throughout George's smile. She slid a napkin across the table. "Maybe just a little, George," she replied. "But just make sure to drink it all up because those smoothies have lots of potassium, which will help with your leg cramps."

"Something's got to help," George said. "Last night, I woke Dawn up twice when I had to jump out of bed—"

"Not a picture I want in my head," interrupted another senior man at the table. "We all know you sleep in the nude." The whir of the blender started up again.

"Sucks getting older, George." Endy patted him on the shoulder as she turned to go. "Say hi to Dawn for me," she said over her shoulder, walking away. "And give kisses to those three Chihuahuas of yours, too."

"I'm not kissing those monsters," George called over the din. "Last time I tried, one of them almost bit my lips off."

Endy giggled and then retreated, heading for her office.

Standing beside the door, a threesome of older ladies, whom everyone called The Grands, bent over a shopping bag they had propped under the plaque that read:

ENDY ANDREWS
Assistant Director of Racquet Sports
Whisper Hills Country Club

"You ladies looking for me?" asked Endy as she came up behind them, causing one to jump.

"Jeez, Endy, you frightened me!" exclaimed Earlene, her eyes wide and her hand on her chest. "I almost had a heart attack."

"—again," said Nora.

"That was a long time ago, Nora. The doctor has given me a clean bill of health since I changed my diet and started exercising," insisted Earlene.

"And you look fantastic," said Endy, placing her hand on Earlene's arm.

Candi adjusted the wide-brimmed hat covering her spiky gray hair. "Sweetie, we were just at the Palm Springs Flea Market, and we found something for you."

"Oh my gosh, you three. That's too—"

Earlene said, "We just wanted to thank you for spending so much time teaching a bunch of old biddies how to play pickleball."

Endy's eyes crinkled. "I mean, they're clinics, and it *is* my job . . ."

Candi reached into the bag and pulled out a neon-green cotton T-shirt. She shook it out, then brought it up to Endy's shoulders, letting it drape across her body. Silk-screened on the front was an illustration of a large green dill pickle wearing Ray Bans and weirdly oversized white gloves and sneakers. The shirt reached past her hips and was so huge that it seemed as if both of them could fit into it at the same time.

Endy blinked, looked down, and read out loud, "Do you pickle?"

Candi hooted with laughter and stepped back, looking Endy up and down. "It's probably a little big for you, but we were lucky to even get this one. Huge mob scene at that table."

Endy gave a pained smile. "I, uh, love it. You gals shouldn't hav—"

"But we did. And guess what else it says on the back," said Nora, her tiny body standing a head shorter than Endy. She motioned for Endy to turn the T-shirt around. Printed across the back in hot pink letters were the words: BIG DINK ENERGY.

"It says, 'Big dink energy,'" whispered Nora with a sly smile.

"I can see that, Nora," replied Endy, biting her lip.

Earlene clapped, and Candi and Nora joined in. "Put it on!" Candi said, and Earlene agreed. "On! On!" chanted Nora, clapping her small, wrinkled hands.

Endy's mouth opened and closed. She chewed the inside of her cheek. And then she took a deep breath, smiling at the trio while she pulled the extra-extra-large neon-green T-shirt over her head. The hem of the T-shirt brushed the bottom of her tennis skirt. She gathered a corner of the shirt and tied it in a knot, adjusting it tightly over her hips.

Twirling in a circle, arms outstretched, Endy laughed. "How do I look?"

"Even more stunning than usual," replied Candi, her hands covering her heart. "Girls, stand next to Endy, and let's get a picture."

Nora moved close to Endy's side. "You can be like me and use the picture for your Tinder profile," she whispered with a slow wink.

3

After The Grands went on their way, Endy sat behind her desk, then logged onto her computer and pulled up an email from Whisper Hills' senior vice president.

The meeting was just a community gathering rather than an official homeowner's association or country club board meeting, so there was no formal agenda, but Endy wanted to be prepared for anything that might spring up.

The monthly meetings were typically attended by a couple dozen club members, some new to Whisper Hills, some who had owned property there since the initial construction in the '80s. Considered the original luxury and leisure spot in the Coachella Valley, Whisper Hills Country Club sat on over 365 acres of meticulously manicured grounds.

Its championship golf courses, twenty-five tennis courts, twenty pickleball courts, two bocce ball lanes, and world-championship croquet lawns were perfectly maintained, tended to daily by an army of landscapers. Diligent attention to detail and impeccable quality were the draw for the thousands of residents who called Whisper Hills home, each of them with an opinion on how the club should be run.

Endy thought back to past meetings where members might grumble about the lack of free coffee in the café, or of the price of the tennis balls they sold in the pro shop. Joel and Endy did what they could to accommodate the requests so the members consistently felt taken care of, but recently there seemed to be more complaining, especially between the tennis and pickleball players.

She glanced at her watch, then grabbed her phone and keys from her desk. She ran through the pro shop, calling over her shoulder to Maria, "I'm late! Taking the golf cart!"

The smell of freshly cut grass and the ongoing drone of lawn mowers filled the air as Endy sped toward the Victor's Clubhouse, located at the heart of the property. She pulled next to the entryway and parked in the slim shade of a towering date palm tree.

Endy stepped up to the Victor's twelve-foot-tall glass double entry doors, which were flanked by huge dark blue ceramic pots filled with sharp-leaved agave and dripping with jasmine vines, their blooms deliciously fragrant. Twin loveseats faced each other across a rug emblazoned with the logo of Whisper Hills Country Club. She pulled open a heavy door and was immediately greeted by the delectable smell of freshly baked bread and grilling meat from the formal dining room's kitchen. On the terrace, Endy saw ladies sitting in the shade of the heavy canvas umbrellas, sipping iced tea and sparkling water, their crystal glasses dewy in the heat.

Endy pushed her sunglasses on top of her head and let her eyes adjust to the dim indoor lighting. "Hey, Amy, am I late?"

The concierge's eyes grew round when she saw Endy walk in wearing the bright dill pickle T-shirt, but she just nodded her head at the meeting room. "Not really, they're just trickling in," she said. "Might be a full room though."

"Thanks," replied Endy. "Would you mind checking in after a bit, just to make sure the AC is keeping up? It's already so hot outside." Endy knew that during these kinds of meetings, feelings and debates on issues could get heated. If they could keep the room chilly, maybe the homeowners would keep their cool.

She entered the room and selected a seat near the door. Whisper Hills' senior vice president and managing director, Daniel York, stood in front of the rows of folding chairs, which were mostly filled. He dressed in typical desert business casual—a bright-colored luxury golf polo shirt and shorts—with his ash-blond hair parted on the side and combed flat. He wore a wide smile and would occasionally point and wink to club members he was friendly with.

"Hello and welcome, everyone," Daniel said. He squinted his eyes at Endy and then indicated to her to close the heavy meeting room door. Chairs scraped the floor, and the whir of the air-conditioning started up as the club members made themselves comfortable.

"I see a lot of friends here, but also some new faces. How about we take a couple of minutes and have our new homeowners stand up and introduce themselves?"

Endy saw an older couple stand up and look around the room. They said they had joined the club for both golf and tennis, so Endy made a note to contact them with news about the racquet club. Four other new members stood up and offered introductions.

Once everyone had settled in their seats again, Daniel went down a checklist he held in his hand, talking about upcoming changes in the restaurant and maintenance around the grounds. Then with ten minutes remaining, he asked if anyone had questions or concerns for open discussion.

An elegant woman with her full, white hair smoothed and pulled back with a thick tortoise-shell barrette raised her hand. She wore a salmon-colored linen tunic and linen trousers, pressed neatly without a wrinkle. Endy saw a vintage Rolex watch on her wrist, and on her finger was a huge pear-shaped diamond ring, stacked on either side with even more diamonds.

Before Daniel could call on her, she asked, "What are you doing about pickleball?" Her voice was sure, steady, and smooth-as-butter.

"Mrs. Tennyson, so nice to see you," said Daniel, giving her a slight bow of his head. "Thanks for asking. Why don't I let our assistant director of racquet sports answer that—Endy?" He held his hand out to Endy, and heads swiveled around toward her.

Endy stood up, looked around the room, and smiled. "Hi, everyone. Yeah, so, pickleball is going great. Our program is growing every week. The daily drop-in matches tend to fill up. We have opportunities for all levels with—"

"That's not what I asked," Barbara Tennyson interrupted. "I asked what are you doing about it."

"About—"

"Yes, about the disruption it has brought to our lovely club." Barbara looked hard at Daniel and then at Endy. "The noise of all those dogs barking and the loud music at all hours of the day. Not to mention that horrendous, nerve-racking sound that plastic ball makes when struck." Endy's eyes went round, and she glanced at Daniel.

He spoke up. "Mrs. Tennyson, I do understand your frustrations with pickleball. Your complaints have not gone unnoticed by the board and me."

Barbara Tennyson huffed. "You've taken away tennis courts."

"Yes, but we still have over twenty-five tennis courts, which is enough for the number of players—"

"That is not the point," she replied with a slow blink. She repeated, "Specifically, you've taken away tennis courts and replaced them with pickleball courts."

"Yes, but—"

"Presidents of the United States would play at Whisper Hills when it was the premier tennis country club in the nation. Why, Jimmy Connors, Martina Navratilova, and so many other tennis professionals called this their home," she said, crossing her hands over her lap.

"Including you and your husband, Clive," added Daniel with a deferential nod.

Barbara stilled and narrowed her eyes at the managing director. "And now those courts have been taken over by something called *pickleball?*"

"Please, Mrs. Tennyson, you must understand what our club needs to do to remain competitive and up-to-date."

"No, Mr. York, it seems that you don't understand. So perhaps I will attend the next board meeting and speak to those who can actually grasp what I'm saying." She stood, smoothed her linen slacks, and calmly headed to the exit. All eyes were on Barbara, and the air in the room was tense. At the door, Barbara paused then looked down her nose at Endy.

"And the club certainly does not need a full-time employee running that sport, when players may simply *drop in*." She pulled open the heavy oak door and exited, a cloud of Chanel No.4 drifting behind her.

"Barbara is not wrong," came a reply from the row of seats. Another club member, Marty Brewer, stood up. "All those golf carts parked at the curbs every day, even with the No Parking Anytime signs. The pickleball players disregard the rules."

Kory Larson raised her hand. "My son is a successful acoustical engineer at Cruz & Cruz Noise Control, and I had him run an analysis on the noise. He said pickleball is louder than my Ninja blender."

A man wearing a Dri-FIT T-shirt and visor chimed in. "Oh come on. You all are complaining about nothing—loosen up. Pickleball is a fun sport."

"But it's louder than a blender," protested Kory. "And my Ninja is so loud that it scares my cats." She looked around the room and said softly, "We can't make margaritas anymore."

Mini arguments broke out amid the crowd.

Daniel said over the din, "Alright, alright. Let's all agree that there are issues with pickleball that the club still needs to work out." He held up his hands, facing the club members. "But, like it or not, pickleball is here to stay. So let's save that discussion for another time."

He indicated for Endy to open the door. "Thank you all for coming. See you next month."

When the room emptied, Daniel rubbed his forehead and walked over to Endy. He let out a big sigh.

"'Big dink energy'?" he asked. "Really?"

Endy's jaw dropped and she slapped a hand on her forehead. "Oh my god, I forgot I was wearing this T-shirt. . . . The Grands just gave it to me as a thank-you gift."

Daniel chuckled. "I was wondering if you'd gotten dressed in the dark this morning."

"Now the tennis members will think that pickleball players are foolish, or worse. I couldn't have made a bigger mistake wearing this silly shirt to this meeting," groaned Endy.

"It's not about you, or even that T-shirt." Daniel sighed. "Just what is it exactly with tennis players that makes them hate pickleball so much? I mean, the sports aren't *that* different."

Endy shrugged, lifting her palms up. "Who knows? Maybe it's like when snowboarders came along. There was so much big hate from the skiers. Remember when some ski hills didn't even allow snowboarders?"

"Yeah, I was one of those snowboarders." Daniel gave a half smile. "Pissed a bunch of people off, for sure."

"Can you imagine if something similar happens where tennis players won't allow pickleball?" Endy mused out loud.

"It's not impossible," replied Daniel. "The only thing that would soothe the animosity is if there was a crossover between tennis and pickleball. Like, look at Jack Sock . . . previously a pro tennis player, now a pro pickleball player."

"Jack Sock?" Endy said with a smile. "One of his social media profiles actually says, 'Used to hit tennis balls. Now dink wiffle balls.' And if that isn't crossover big dink energy, I'm not sure what is."

4

Endy was still puzzled as she climbed back onto the pro shop's golf cart. She didn't know why tennis players loathed pickleball, but she was sure of pickleball's growing popularity.

Heading back to work, she decided to take the long way and loop past all the courts. It was another glorious day with a searing sun and cloudless sky, and the wind swirled around her in the open-air cart.

At the far end of the racquet property, many of the pickleball courts were filled. On one court, a mother and young son were playing against a father and even younger son. A stroller parked in the shade held an infant who had just started screaming. On the next court over, The Grands played with a fourth player, who cackled loudly with delight when she hit a winning shot between Candi and Nora.

Endy tooted the golf cart's horn, leaned out, and waved. Candi held up her hand, shading her eyes, then yelled out, "Hiiiii, Ennnnnddddyyyy!"

Endy's gaze then shifted to the tennis courts across from the pickleball courts. A middle-aged foursome was immersed in their tennis match, their slow, sure steps gliding from side to side and moving deliberately forward to the net. Dressed in white, they seemed like the occasional groups of egrets that glided above the country club's golf course lakes.

"Well done," one called out. The only other sound coming from their court was the pop of the felted tennis ball against the strings of their racquets.

As Endy drove past, she couldn't help but compare the two sports being played next to each other. Daniel had said that they weren't *that* different. But Endy knew that to some people, tennis and pickleball were as different as cats and dogs.

She slowed the golf cart as a bright green plastic ball rolled onto the path. She parked and picked up the ball and walked in the direction of the courts, looking around for its owner.

As she passed in between the pickleball court and the tennis court directly next to it, Endy's gaze was drawn to two younger tennis players. The one with short black hair was Collin Park, a club member in his late twenties.

But who was the other one? He was lean and muscular with his tousled brown hair pulled back with a headband. Endy couldn't pull her eyes away. She inhaled sharply as he turned to return a serve, revealing his face—it was the drop-dead gorgeous guy who'd rescued Rusty.

Endy leaned on the fence, her hair flowing over her shoulders. She pushed her sunglasses up on top of her head and watched, riveted, as the tennis battle played out. The ball rocketed back and forth between the immensely skilled players, each hitting it so hard that the boom of the ball off their racquets echoed like fireworks on the Fourth of July.

On the next point, Collin hit a huge, whomping serve. But the handsome stranger returned the ball as if it were nothing more than a feather floating in the air, hitting it so solidly, so deeply, that it landed inches away from the baseline before Collin had any chance of moving.

"Nice shot, Hall," called Collin, clapping his hand on the strings of his racquet.

Endy leaned back from the fence and applauded. When Rusty's rescuer glanced up to the railing, she thought she saw him grin.

On the next point, Collin was incapable of handling a returned hard-hit ball, and it popped up, way above his head. He shook his head and muttered, "Crap," when he realized that his ball would be an easy slam return. The handsome stranger lifted his left arm, pointing to the sky, his right arm cocked behind him.

But from the side of the court, another ball, this one bright green plastic with holes, sailed onto the tennis court just as he swung overhead and slammed the tennis ball . . . right into the net.

The plastic pickleball rolled onto the court—its thin and reedy *clk, clk, clk, clk* sounding loud in the absolute stillness of the aftermath of the netted overhead slam—and came to rest against his foot.

"Ball on!" shouted an older pickleball player wearing a purple flowered shade hat, her palms on her cheeks. "Sorry!" She ran over from her pickleball court, horrified.

On the opposite side of the tennis court, Collin stood, a look of annoyance across his face and his racquet lowered by his side. But the handsome stranger just took a deep breath and adjusted the headband holding back his tangled mane of dark, chocolate-brown hair. He rolled his neck and shoulders in irritation, picked up the pickleball, and tossed it up in the air.

"Someone missing this?" he asked. Then he swatted the plastic ball, launching it with velocity out of the tennis court.

Endy stepped aside quickly, stumbling back, barely dodging the pickleball as it came shooting toward her head.

Sebastian Hall pushed back his dark brown hair again. After netting that shot, he'd looked up to see where that miserable bright green plastic ball came from. At first, he'd only seen a huge neon-green T-shirt with something that looked like a dill pickle wearing Ray Bans and weirdly oversized white gloves across the front. But then he saw her watching from the fence, with the sun from behind, creating a radiant halo around her. A shock of long, dark hair hung down her back and shadows brought out the lean and athletic cut of her arms. Her legs, long and graceful, peaked out from under a short tennis skirt. Sebastian grinned when he recognized her as the girl from earlier, when he'd pulled that vicious dog out from under the bush and scratched his hand.

He studied her, standing at the railing, and within seconds, he took in her striking eyes that were rimmed with thick, dark lashes and had a slight upturn at the outside edges. But it was her mouth, opened into a gasp when she'd realized he'd missed that easy overhead, that stuck in his mind. *A mouth*, he thought, *that was infinitely kissable.*

"TIME!" yelled Collin from the other side of the net, holding up his hands. "If I could, I'd give you a freakin' time violation. Serve it up, already!"

"What do you mean 'time violation'?" yelled Sebastian, laughing. He held one tennis ball and shoved another in the pocket of his shorts. "What are you, an actual player or a chair umpire?"

Collin shook his head, a huge grin across his face. "Just serve, Hall."

"Alright, Park," Sebastian agreed. "You asked for it."

He took the tennis ball in his left hand, tossed it high above his head, loaded up on his back leg, then exploded up. His racquet carved through the air, the strings making contact with the fuzzy green ball. It soared over the net at about a hundred miles per hour, then hit the front of the service line, and blasted directly into Collin's body.

Twisting his hips to avoid getting hit, Collin blocked the serve with his racquet, which sent the ball flying high in the sky. Sebastian jogged toward the net, leaped into the air with his racquet cocked behind him, and slammed the ball. It ricocheted off the hard surface and flew over the ten-foot-high chain-link fence, finally coming to a stop yards away on the nearby manicured croquet court.

Sebastian landed on his feet, laughing.

He looked up at the railing to see if the stunning girl with the long, dark hair saw *that* overhead slam, but she'd vanished, only leaving him with an image of a huge neon-green T-shirt with a dill pickle.

5

Refolding a stack of T-shirts with Whisper Hills logos and placing them at the edge of the table, Endy recounted what had gone on during the community meeting earlier in the day. She moved around the shop, tidying it up after closing.

"... and like Daniel said, pickleball is here to stay," said Endy. "Especially since it's starting to appeal to younger players."

Maria bunched up the cloth she'd been using to dust the racks and glanced up at the wall clock. She said, "Speaking of younger players, you better get going or you'll be late again."

Endy looked at her phone, checking the time. "Dammit, I can't be late again! The kids don't have adult supervision until I—"

The telephone on the front desk rang, the sound piercing in the empty pro shop. They slid glances at each other and then to the ringing telephone.

"Should we—" started Endy.

Maria shook her head. "No, we're closed. Don't answer it—"

"Hello, Whisper Hills racquet pro shop," said Endy, after lifting the receiver to her ear. "Hey, Gary, what can I do for you?" Maria rolled her eyes and pointed at the clock.

Endy shrugged with her palm in the air. "Hang on one sec while I pull up my schedule. . . . I'm going to put you on hold." She pressed a button on the phone and looked at Maria, her eyes pleading.

"Alright, alright. I gotchu," said Maria, walking to the front desk. She tucked the cloth into a drawer and withdrew her key ring. "I'll head over now, but I'm literally not doing anything until you get there, and you owe me for this." She opened the door and called over her shoulder, "I'm locking the door behind me. Get there as soon as you can."

"Thanks, I'll pay you back, I promise!" replied Endy as she pressed the hold button again. "Gary, you still there?"

After she'd hung up the phone, Endy looked at the clock and saw how late she was. She ran to her office, grabbed her purse and keys, and flicked off the lights. With the sun setting behind the mountains, the pro shop windows darkened. Endy took one last look over the shop, making sure everything was in order. She unlocked the glass door, flung it open, stepped through, and ran smack into something solid. Someone solid.

Strong arms wrapped around her, preventing her from toppling down the steps.

"Gah!" she shrieked. Her face pressed into a firm chest, the top of her head reaching just below a strong chin.

"Did you just say 'gah'?" the extremely handsome guy holding her asked, his tone full of amusement. Endy looked up to thick lashes surrounding intense light blue eyes staring deep into hers. Her heart thudded in her chest, and she seemed to have quit breathing all the while his arms held her in a warm, protective embrace.

"Did I?" she stammered, gathering herself and stepping back from him. Her eyes widened when she recognized him as Rusty's rescuer and Collin Park's tennis opponent from just a few hours before, and her heart skipped more than a beat.

"I'm so sorry. I'm late and—" Her cell phone dinged with an incoming text from Maria:

> WHERE R U??? KIDS R RIOTING

"The shop is actually closed, and I'm late. I'm so sorry," she stammered, tripping over her words. "I'm late."

Looking thoughtful, he rubbed his smooth chin, the gesture sending shivers along Endy's arms. Why was it that when incredibly handsome men rubbed their chins, it made women feel faint?

"Can you come back tomorrow morning? We open at seven o'clock," she choked out.

He looked at her from the side of his eyes. "Sure, tomorrow," he replied. He flashed the same smile he had earlier, the sexy, crooked one that had her tummy all aflutter. "It's a date." He took a step back as Endy pulled the door shut.

She could feel his eyes on her as she locked the door behind her. She smoothed back her hair and couldn't help but tug her tennis skirt farther down her slender hips. Jogging away, Endy was very aware that the extremely attractive guy standing under the pro shop awning was still watching her as she disappeared around the corner.

6

They really were rioting, or so it seemed to Endy when she finally got to the pickleball courts. Kids ran around the close-clipped lawn, chasing, screaming, and throwing balls at each other. Others crowded around a cell phone watching a TikTok dance video, with a couple of kids attempting to copy it but instead looking like they were being delivered electrical shocks.

Endy slid a look to Maria. "You couldn't have gotten them started?"

"I'm just here covering for you, *mi reina*, my queen. I told you not to answer that call," she replied, swatting at the air. "This completely nutty mess is yours, not mine."

"You're right, Maria." Endy burst out laughing and twirled around with her arms in the air. "This big, beautiful, nutty mess is mine."

When Endy had arrived in the Coachella Valley two years prior, pickleball was still fairly new. But the new sport had seduced plenty of players and fans, and it quickly exploded in popularity, especially among the Boomers and Gen Xers who lived in the desert area.

Sensing an opportunity that did not previously exist for younger generations, Endy put together a plan for a Palm Springs youth pickleball program for kids eighteen and under. Maria told her aunt, a principal at one of the Palm Springs public schools, about Endy's plan. And it turned out that the school actually needed an extracurricular program for kids who didn't have after-school opportunities, didn't fit in with traditional sports clubs, or couldn't afford private sports lessons.

Endy's plan would take a couple of years to establish, while relying on Whisper Hills Country Club as a host and sponsor. It would introduce pickleball to the kids and their parents and raise Whisper Hills' profile in the local community. And at the end of the two years, Endy would hand the school a fully formed after-school pickleball program.

She'd presented the idea to Joel, who then suggested it to Daniel York. Almost immediately, her introductory pickleball program was adopted. Whisper Hills had given her a two-year monetary fund for snacks and drinks, paddles and balls, and also donated their courts for the period.

She called it Picklers Youth Pickleball League. And it was a hit.

Everywhere she went, someone would inevitably stop her and tell her how much their child loved Picklers. Mothers would get out of their cars during pickup, run over to Endy, and hug her hard, sometimes bringing her Tupperware containers filled with home-cooked meals. Even most of the staff around Whisper Hills knew that Endy ran the program and would call out to her and wave when they'd roll past the courts full of kids in the afternoons.

Endy made sure the program was free to all kids, and in the couple of years since she started Picklers, it had grown from six kids to sixty, a certifiable success.

Two years had gone by quickly, and Joel had approached Endy, wanting to discuss the Picklers' initial term expiring. They'd sat in the shade on the pro shop's patio, overlooking Stadium Court and the beautiful, deep-green grass croquet courts.

"Daniel wanted me to tell you congratulations on the success of Picklers," said Joel, taking a sip of his mixed berry acai smoothie.

Endy smiled. "Thanks . . . I can't wait to see what we do these next couple of years."

Joel's eyebrows drew together over his mirrored aviator sunglasses. "Next couple of years?" He frowned. "Endy, did you forget that the club only agreed for two years?"

"No, I haven't forgotten, but—"

"The school is supposed to take it over in a couple of months," Joel reminded her.

"I know, but Maria's aunt was hoping Whisper Hills could keep it going. She said that with the cuts in the after-school programming budget, there is no way the school can pay for Picklers."

"I was just at the club's annual budget meetings, and well, neither can we," replied Joel. "Picklers isn't in the budget for the future."

"Dammit!" grumbled Endy. "Joel, do you think I can change Daniel's mind . . . have him go back over the budget and put Picklers back in?"

"I doubt it, Endy. Daniel had actually allocated Picklers around $25,000 for the past two years," replied Joel. "That's a lot of money. Especially for a program that you're supposed to hand over to a public school."

Endy frowned, crestfallen. "Well, the school can't come up with that kind of money either." She covered her face with her hands. "Oh nooo . . . Does that mean this will be the end of Picklers?"

"Unless you can come up with the money for the next couple of years." Joel shrugged and then looked far over to the pickleball courts filled with players. "I don't know, maybe . . ."

Endy peeked through her hands, her eyebrows raised.

"Like maybe if you wanted to do a fundraiser out of the racquet club before the end of the season, we could help you out with that at least." He took a sip of his smoothie. "We could do a Saturday event or something."

"Oh my gosh, that's awesome. A Saturday fundraising event!" exclaimed Endy, bouncing in her seat. "Great idea. Thank you so much, Joel."

"Don't thank me yet . . . it's all on your shoulders. It'll be completely up to you to raise the $25,000," replied Joel. "You think you'll be able to do that?"

Endy nodded and smiled widely. "Anything can happen."

Endy rounded up all the kids and separated them four to a court. With an even number of kids, all of them could play and no one would need to sit out. Endy went over the rules, reminding the kids to play fair.

"... and if a ball lands on the very outside of a line, is it considered in or out?" she asked the group.

"If *I* hit it, then it's in," came a reply. "If it's anyone else's, then it's out."

Endy rolled her eyes but smiled at the boy holding the paddle next to her. Ten-year-old Paco Lopez had been one of the first to join up with Picklers. His mother worked a midday shift, so he always found his own way to Whisper Hills on the bus after school. His older brothers were athletic and participated in competitive organized sports throughout the year, but Paco was considered too impulsive, too volatile, and too much of a handful, so he never lasted long with any team or coach. Paco just wasn't made for team sports.

Endy once had overheard Paco describe himself as "short, fat, and brown," which, unfortunately, Endy could not disagree with. Paco kept his jet-black hair cropped short, close to his large, round head, a little cowlick swirling at his crown. His cheeks plumped his face, surrounding his dark eyes, hooded with heavy lids.

The wicked gleam in his eyes, along with his arrogance, set him apart from the rest of the kids in the program. On and off the pickleball court, if he were ever provoked in the slightest, his response would often cause exasperation or even tears. Yet, minutes or even seconds afterward, Paco would be apologetic, offering his hand to whomever he'd upset. He'd give a full smile and would be attentive the rest of the practice time.

Was it bluster or was it charisma that made him so unpredictable? Endy thought that maybe with Paco, they were one and the same.

Paco's mother, Valentina, picked him up after she got off work at seven o'clock, but she often ran late, giving Endy alone time with Paco. It didn't take Endy long to see that there was something magical about Paco, and she wondered if anyone else would ever see that too.

The kids played hard over the course of the next hour as the afternoon began transitioning to early evening. At the end of the last point, laughing and yelling and talking, they all drifted off the courts to the tables scattered with water and Gatorade bottles and backpacks. When the sun started drifting lower, dropping below the tops of the palm trees, and the air grew chilly, some kids pulled hoodies over their heads. They moved onto the lawn, waiting for the Toyotas, Hyundais, and Kias driven by a mother or older sibling to pull up to bring them home.

"Look!" a little girl said, her face tilted upward.

Above them, dozens of Canada geese soared over the courts, their wings beating along with their honking calls. The kids, inexplicably and finally hushed, lifted their eyes. The large birds in their V formation seemed like an arrow cutting across the entire periwinkle sky. They all watched mesmerized.

Pushing past the other kids close to Endy, Paco took a spot right next to her, then reached out and placed his small, sweaty hand in hers until the geese flapped away, their honks fading into the night.

7

Sebastian knew it was creepy to follow her after she had locked up the pro shop and raced away. But leaning into his bad decision, he started his own golf cart and tailed Endy, keeping a block behind her.

After she had bumped into him, as he held her in his arms, he had instantly felt a mega-spark of attraction. And when she'd turned around and jogged off and he saw "Big Dink Energy" printed on the back of her huge neon-green T-shirt, Sebastian had actually laughed out loud.

He didn't know her, but he knew he wanted to.

Big time.

He'd followed her around the perimeter of the racquet club's tennis courts to where she joined a group of wild and out-of-control kids. She had stepped in the middle of that chaos and let loose with the most joyous laugh. Watching her twirl, her long, dark hair fanning out behind her, had Sebastian bewitched.

All of the kids seemed to love her—the young ones ran around her, screaming, while the older ones walked next to her, their faces upturned with relaxed smiles.

But when she'd gotten all the kids out onto pickleball courts and they had started hitting the bright green wiffle ball, Sebastian knew it was his cue to move on. Sure, maybe pickleball was picking up across the nation, but it wasn't at all for him, and the sound of those stupid paddles hitting those annoying plastic balls was quickly getting on his nerves.

Sebastian clicked the switch on the golf cart to drive forward and cranked the steering wheel into a U-turn. He looked over his shoulder one last time and saw her under the awning, bent over the picnic table. He tapped on the cart's accelerator and slowly rolled away just as he heard some Harry Styles song from the speaker on the table. Looking back, he saw the girl tug her short tennis skirt over her hips again.

He cruised around the country club slowly, enjoying the end-of-day quiet. The landscaping crew had gone home hours before, so calm had settled over the lush green golf courses. Smooth as mirrors, the water of the ponds reflected the last rays of the sun dipping behind the San Jacinto Mountains. Someone grilled steaks on their back patio, the smell making Sebastian's stomach growl.

Heading home, Sebastian took the road next to the pickleball courts, where the kids were all now waiting on the nearby grass. Evening was just coming on, and he didn't yet need to put on the headlights. So he parked in the same place he had earlier, a block away, and watched the kids gather around the girl in the "Big Dink Energy" T-shirt.

He heard a little girl yell, "Look!" Then he saw a massive flock of gray-and-brown geese cruising above them all in a huge wedge-shaped V. Echoing off the walls of the Spanish-style homes, their nasal *hooonks* seemed to strum through his bones.

He inhaled and then blew out a thin stream. "Whoa," he whispered, captivated. He didn't know the last time he'd seen anything so achingly breathtaking.

But then Sebastian saw that chonker of a little dude push his way next to the beautiful girl in the neon T-shirt and slip his hand into hers. . . . Well, that tugged at his heartstrings so much that it just about killed him.

8

Endy stood next to the patio railing overlooking the entirety of the racquet club. In front of her, four couples dressed in all white played croquet on the world-famous lawns that had hosted many national and international croquet tournaments. Directly in front of the deep-green clipped lawn was the sunken stadium tennis court, lined with seating. To her right were the lesson and practice courts, where both tennis ball machines were in use, shooting balls toward the pros and young amateurs with a sound like a thudding *pop*. To her left were the dozens of tennis hard courts next to the many pickleball courts, filled and boisterous as usual. But farther out, just past it all were Whisper Hills' famed grass tennis courts. These were the only grass courts in the area, and they were meticulously maintained, clipped tight like carpet, and striped with gleaming white chalk. The grass was especially favored by the older tennis crowd because of its more forgiving impact on players' bodies.

The door to the pro shop flung open, and Maria rushed

outside to Endy, a bag of ice in her hand. "Joel just called. Looks like another injury, and he needs this ice right away."

Endy grabbed it from Maria's hands. "Which court?" she asked, already moving from the patio.

"Grass court one," replied Maria.

"Grass?" Endy turned, questioning. "Not pickleball?"

"Pickleball already has a torn rotator cuff and a snapped wrist this week. About time tennis took a turn."

Endy ran down the steps and jumped into her golf cart. By the time she arrived, she could see Joel bent over someone sitting on the grass court, one leg stretched out.

"Hey," she called out. "You needed ice?" She strode toward them.

Joel stepped aside, and Endy looked down at the player on the ground. She inhaled sharply. Sitting on the grass was the extremely handsome guy she'd seen playing against Collin Park. The same guy who had rescued Rusty. The one with the gorgeous brown hair and intense light blue eyes that belonged to . . . the one she'd slammed into the day before when she'd darted out of the pro shop because she was late.

"Are you okay?" she stammered.

"Well, now that you're here," he said, his full lips pulled up on one side, "more than okay."

Endy's heart pounded in her throat. She froze in front of them, the bag of ice dripping down her leg.

"Could I have that? Or did you want to keep it for yourself?" he asked, a smile still playing on his lips.

"Oh my gosh, of course. Here." She stuck out her hand and then stood still, her eyes wide, her heart still skipping.

Joel crossed his arms and looked from Endy down to the injured player. "Uh, Sebastian, this is Endy Andrews, our assistant director of racquet sports." He lifted his chin toward Endy as an introduction.

Joel's eyes shifted between the two, sensing a chemistry between them, and a sour expression crossed his face. The sound of tinkling wind chimes from the yard across the street carried to them in the warm breeze.

"Endy, this is Sebastian Hall. We were just hitting, and he turned his knee after I aced him."

"That was not an ace," groaned Sebastian. "Your ball was so out, it wasn't even close to being near the line."

"So why'd you lunge for it?"

"That was not an ace," repeated Sebastian.

"My signature shots have always been out wide, painting the lines." Joel smiled, relishing the argument. "It *absolutely* was an ace."

"Bullshit," replied Sebastian.

"So, then why'd you try to return it?" Joel asked, laughing.

Sebastian rolled his eyes and then held out his hand to Endy. "Help me get over to the bench?" She grasped his strong hand in hers and a shock of electricity jolted between them.

In a fluid move, Sebastian got up from the grass and stood, gingerly testing his injured knee. He was a head taller than Endy, with long legs and broad shoulders. His dark brown, chin-length hair was again pulled back with an elastic headband, accentuating his high cheekbones. And his eyes . . . they were hypnotic.

Joel shoved himself between Sebastian and Endy. He took

Sebastian by the arm, leading him off the grass. "Dude, I'll help you," Joel grumbled and slid a glance at Endy.

From the edge of the grass court, two dogs got into a barking, snarling skirmish and lunged at each other while their owners yanked at their leashes, trying to keep them separate. With the jealous way that Joel was acting, Endy hoped that she wouldn't have to pull him and Sebastian apart as well.

"Do you need to go to the urgent care clinic?" asked Endy, following them off the court. She pulled her phone out of her pocket. "I can find someone to take you over to Eisenhower."

"No, thanks though. This is an old injury that keeps haunting me. Unfortunately, I'm used to reinjuring it." Sebastian lowered himself onto the bench. "I'll just ice it for a bit, then I should be fine to get home and elevate it." He shifted on the bench and then tilted his head up, looking at Endy with a small smile. His eyes held hers.

Endy felt her face redden. She bit at her lip and shrugged one shoulder. "Well, I guess if you're really okay, I should get back to the shop."

"Yeah, you should," said Joel, his eyes narrowed. "And hey, since you're going past court eleven, can you tell—"

"Actually, I'm not sure I can make it on my own to my car," interrupted Sebastian. He looked up through his thick eyelashes at Endy. "Could you maybe help me out?" A perfect smile pulled at his lips, and Endy felt faint.

"Sebastian, I can help you get to your car," volunteered Joel, eyeing them.

"That's okay, Joel. I know you're supposed to be teaching another lesson right now. She . . ." He looked from face to face.

"Endy," she reminded him, trying to calm her pounding heart.

Sebastian smiled again. "Endy can help me."

The golf cart was close enough that Sebastian could have hobbled there on his own, but he had insisted on putting his arm around Endy's shoulders for support. She thought that she'd done the best she could in assisting him, even though she was already weak in her knees from just being near him. But once they'd maneuvered into the cart and her pounding heart had settled, Endy still had to grasp the steering wheel tightly to hide her shaking hands.

Endy's cell phone rang, causing her to jump in her seat. She saw Sebastian bring his hand up to his mouth to hide a grin.

"Hey, Maria," she said, smiling and putting her phone on speaker. "What's up?" Endy turned on the golf cart and slowly pulled onto the gravel path.

"You're not going to like this, but could you check on the pickleball courts?" asked Maria.

"Yeah, sure. Why?"

"Mr. Brewer just came in here yelling about the pickleballers next to his tennis court. He's on court eight and—"

". . . it's right next to the pickleball courts." Endy frowned. "I'm on my way." She hung up her call and turned to Sebastian. "I have a bit of an emergency. Do you mind if we make a stop?"

"No problem. Let's get over there," said Sebastian, shaking his head. "Step on it, Lightning McQueen."

Endy's eyebrows rose and she smiled. She floored the accelerator, the surge throwing Sebastian back into his seat. He burst out laughing and grabbed hold of the armrest. Endy laughed too and took a sharp corner. "You *told* me to step on it."

They arrived just as an argument broke out between two middle-aged men who stood on the strip of lawn between the pickleball and tennis courts.

"Keep that goddamn stupid wiffle ball on your own court!" yelled Marty Brewer.

"Jesus, Marty, calm down."

"Don't you tell me to calm down. I'm sick and tired of our tennis games getting interrupted by all of your foolishness. It's not just the incessant noise anymore. Now that you all are encroaching on our tennis courts, we have to deal with these stupid plastic balls stopping our play."

Endy left Sebastian sitting in the golf cart and ran toward Marty and George. She lifted her hands up, palms out, and patted at the air. "Hey, you two. Can I help out here?"

"Oh, Endy," said Marty, exasperated. "This pickleball thing is just ruining everything."

George interrupted and said with sarcasm, "Ohhh, *pickleball is just ruining everything*. Marty, just slither out of the ice age and get used to the idea that pickleball is getting more popular than tennis."

Endy saw Marty grit his teeth and his face turn red.

"Okay, okay. Can someone tell me what's happened?" she asked.

George stepped forward and gestured at the pickleball court where three other players stood uncomfortably. "We were on game point, Terry popped up a dink, I hit a flawless overhead slam which bounced high and sent the ball over the fence and onto their court." He glanced at Marty. "Simple mistake."

"Not so simple when it was the third time it happened in an hour!" yelled Marty. "We had match point, and as I served, this stupid ball bounced onto our court." He threw the bright green plastic ball at George, hitting him on the forehead. "I'm over this. Something's got to be done." Marty stormed away. "Something *will* be done," he said over his shoulder.

George wiggled his head and rolled his eyes. And then he raised both hands and slowly flipped up his middle fingers to Marty's retreating back.

He turned to Endy. "Sorry for the trouble, Endy." He grinned and shrugged his shoulders. "Can George Jacobs help it if his overhead slams are flawless?"

Endy returned to Sebastian sitting in the back seat of the golf cart, his leg propped up with the bag of ice melting around his knee. He looked like he was trying to fight back a smile. Endy couldn't help herself and she bit at her lips trying to hide her grin too, but when their eyes locked, they both burst out laughing.

"That George is a feisty old dude," remarked Sebastian. "But you know he's wrong. I mean, if I were serving for the match and I lost because a ball interrupted me, I'd be pissed."

"Yeah, I can imagine." Endy nodded, remembering the day before when she'd seen Sebastian playing with Collin Park. "But you know what? I'm never going to understand why there is such big hate between tennis players and pickleball players."

She tilted her head and studied Sebastian. A loud beeping came from a delivery van backing up in the parking lot.

"So," she asked, "which side are you on?"

Sebastian pursed his lips, his eyes appraising Endy. "Sebastian Hall. Tennis."

He raised his chin. "You?"

Endy raised one eyebrow. "Endy Andrews. Pickleball." She crossed her arms over her chest and leaned against the golf cart.

Sebastian grinned, then raised both hands and slowly flipped up his middle fingers at Endy. And with that, they both dissolved into laughter.

9

After Endy brought Sebastian to the parking lot, she helped him limp to his car. She couldn't help but feel like he was faking the need for her assistance a little. But in all honesty, she didn't mind one single bit and was maybe taking her time getting him settled into the driver's seat.

She held on to the door and roof while Sebastian used her shoulder for support in sliding into the car. His handprint burned through the strap of her Dri-FIT tank top, and Endy felt she might go up in flames.

After Sebastian adjusted his seat, Endy stepped back and started swinging the door shut, but Sebastian held it open with an arm, his biceps bulging from his T-shirt sleeve. "So . . . what do assistant directors of racquet sports do after work?" he asked with a slow smile.

Endy felt the blood rise up her neck to her face and her heart pounded again. "Oh, well, I need to put some time into the Picklers fundraiser, and I have about fifty unanswered emails, and—"

"I said *after* work. And I didn't mean for the rest of the year." Sebastian grinned. "I was kind of wondering about, like, tonight."

"Tonight?" stammered Endy.

"Yeah, I'm just here visiting for a while, and I don't really know very many people," replied Sebastian. "I'm kind of bored of my own company."

"You know Joel," Endy asserted.

Sebastian laughed. "I'm not *that* bored of my own company."

Endy bit her bottom lip.

"I mean, we've bumped into each other four times. That's either random or you're some kind of creepy stalker."

"I'm not a creepy stalker!" Endy exclaimed. The butterflies in her stomach went berserk. Sebastian was keeping track of how many times they'd met? Did he also feel the connection and attraction between them?

"I'll be the judge of that." Sebastian chuckled. "Come on. I'll swing by here at five o'clock," he said.

And then he looked at her so earnestly, so intensely with those extraordinary light blue eyes that Endy couldn't refuse.

"See you at five," she said, smiling, looking at Sebastian, and tucking a strand of hair behind her ear.

Sebastian waited outside the pro shop, in the driver's seat of his own golf cart, his knee wrapped tightly in a supportive brace. Endy felt her face light up as she approached the cart, and she spied two folding lounge chairs and a small cooler in the back.

This was her favorite time of the day, when the sun was lowering behind the San Jacinto Mountains, the clouds were glowing pink and purple, and the *ssssssh-chk-chk-chk* of the sprinklers could be heard watering the grass tennis courts.

"Since I can't really walk anywhere, I thought we could just take a drive."

"Sounds wonderful." Endy smiled as she climbed into the passenger seat. "Do you have a place in mind, or can I suggest one?"

"Like I said, I'm just a visitor, so by all means." Sebastian put the golf cart in reverse. "You might want to hold on." He stepped on the accelerator, throwing her off balance and making her grab hold of the dashboard, sending Endy into a giggling fit.

At the farthest end of the country club's land, the cart climbed a small hill and then came to a rest. Looking northeast toward mountains shadowed in gray-blue, they watched a freight train crossing in the distance, pulling car after car loaded with huge metal shipping containers. Around them, towering palm trees reached sky-high, their fronds trembling. Sebastian and Endy breathed in the dry, dusty air, the sultry breeze caressing their skin.

While Endy was taking in the view, she felt Sebastian's eyes on her and she felt her face flush again. She popped up from the passenger seat and turned her head away from Sebastian, willing her blush to fade.

"Here, let me set these up." She lifted the chairs and cooler, then placed them facing the view.

Sebastian hauled himself from the golf cart and then limped to a chair, lowering his strong, lean body down. He reached out to the cooler, lifted up the top, and pulled out a bottle of wine. He handed it to Endy and then pulled out two plastic cups, a sheepish look across his face, but Endy just uncorked the bottle and poured.

"Classy," Endy teased, eyeing the plastic cup. She took a sip, then smiled, appreciating the wine Sebastian had chosen. "Hey, this is actually really good. Very sweet of you to bring it."

Sebastian pulled the cooler closer, then propped his foot on top. "It's more for the pain in my knee," he said, grimacing.

"You're sure milking that injury," Endy replied with a twinkle in her eye.

"What, you've never had an injury?" asked Sebastian.

"Not rea—"

"—maybe hurt your face?"

"My face?"

"Because it's killin' me," Sebastian finished, chuckling and eliciting a groan from Endy. They continued joking around, keeping the conversation light, until the bottle of wine was empty.

Music drifted on the warm breeze from a cover band at the nearby Marriott playing "Brown Eyed Girl." Sebastian quietly sang along, his voice smooth. And when Endy looked up and caught Sebastian's warm gaze, her lips lifted in a small smile.

Sebastian reached over and put his hand on Endy's leg. "Maybe we can do this again. Sometime soon." He squeezed her knee softly, causing goose bumps to erupt across her entire body.

Endy worried when she recognized the fluttery feeling . . . the feeling of falling head over heels for someone. Seriously, how could she already be so smitten with Sebastian when they'd only been around each other for a few hours?

The answer was obvious. Sebastian was dreamy. Besides those mesmerizing light blue eyes rimmed with his dark eyelashes, and his mop of tousled, chocolate-brown hair that caressed his cheeks and curled around his ears, the way he carried himself was just plain sexy.

Even with an injured knee, his body moved with a fluidness that seemed almost animal-like. When he lowered himself into the camp chair, his arms had taken the brunt of his weight, and she'd once again noticed his strong biceps straining the sleeves of his T-shirt. Endy felt her breath hitch when she thought about what those arms and biceps would look like if he were holding her hips.

"Yeah, maybe we can do this again sometime soon," she repeated, trying to be casual, but fighting the urge to tumble blindly into love.

Endy's last relationship—the big one, the long one, the important one, the one with Bennett—had started with her tumbling blindly into love. But when it ended, the heartbreak it caused her was immense. So much so that Endy had vowed to never ever again let herself fall for someone so hard and fast.

And that's what had her worried now with Sebastian.

10

Fingers snapped in front of her face, startling her from her reverie. Endy blinked quickly and found herself at the water dispenser in the hallway near the gym, holding her bottle under the spigot, the cold water almost cresting and overflowing.

"Someone is in la-la land," said Paul Rothman, his eyebrows raised. He nudged her away from the cooler and started filling his tumbler. "If you're anything like me, you're either thinking about the sexy new golf pro the club just hired . . . or what you're going to have for lunch."

Endy giggled and turned to Paul with a wide smile. "Neither," she replied. "But not far off."

"Ooh, do tell." Paul sipped from the straw poking out of the lid of his tumbler.

"There's really nothing to—"

"Liar," Paul said accusingly with a pout. "But it becomes you. Makes you seem mysterious."

Endy blew a kiss to Paul as she walked away. He was one of her favorite members at Whisper Hills. In fact, he was a favorite among many of the club's employees. Well-known for his clever wit as well as his generosity, Paul seemed to make every situation simply a bit better.

A couple of years earlier, when Endy had just started as the brand-new assistant director of racquet sports at Whisper Hills, she was surprised to receive an invitation to a happy hour gathering at Gary Lombardi and Dean Fuller's home. After all, she'd only been on the job for a few weeks. But never one to pass up an opportunity to network with the possibility of good food and drink, Endy readily accepted the invitation.

She'd walked into the entryway, pushed the heavy dark-wood door closed behind her, and then walked through to the open kitchen and dining area. It took her eyes a moment to adjust to the late afternoon light glaring through the wall of windows along the back. A large basket holding pots of delicate white orchids sat in the center of the dining room table, plates of appetizers surrounding it. Cher's deep, weighty voice sang softly over the home's built-in speakers. Dozens of guests stood outside, near an inviting pool, the fountain spray drowning out their conversations.

"Hi, I don't believe we've actually met yet," said Paul Rothman, approaching Endy with his hand outstretched. "I'm Paul. Gary and Dean are out back, so I'm doing their work in greeting their guests. Typical."

Endy smiled and switched the bottle of wine she brought to her left hand, reaching out her right to shake Paul's. "Nice to meet you, Paul."

After grasping Endy's hand and looking at the wine she held, Paul's lips pursed. "*Organic* wine?" he asked, looking aghast. "You're not one of those, are you?"

Endy's eyebrows rose, and she looked puzzled. "One of those . . . ?"

"Vegan," whispered Paul, looking over his shoulder. "Not that there's anything wrong with that."

Endy laughed. "I'm not a vegan, and yes, the wine is organic. I went to a wine tasting recently, and we all loved this pinot grigio."

"Oh, well I do love a good pinot grigio."

"Then you'll like this one. Especially paired with those delicious looking carne asada nachos on the table."

Paul glanced toward the dining room table. "I loved a vegan once, but it didn't work out." He patted his thick belly. "It seems that I loved carne asada more."

They spent the rest of the party together, with Paul introducing Endy to all the guests. By the end of the gathering, Endy had her following week completely booked with people signed up for group and individual pickleball lessons. And she and Paul developed a great friendship.

Still standing by the water dispenser, Paul called out to Endy's retreating back, "See you tomorrow at the clinic." She raised her hand and gave a thumbs-up as the clank of the weight machines followed her down the hallway.

Paul turned from the water station, mopped the sweat from his neck with a towel, and surveyed the workout room. The Grands were grouped in the far corner. Candi, her spiky gray hair standing straight out, steadied herself with the wall-mounted bar as she lifted her knee high to her chest. Earlene sat on a yoga mat with a pair of reading glasses perched on her nose, crisscrossed her legs, then rested her wrists across them. And Nora stood at the mirror, staring at her reflection and scrubbing at her mouth with a tissue, removing lipstick staining her teeth.

Sebastian sat at a weight machine on the opposite side of the gym, rhythmically bending his knee up and down.

"Hey, Paul," Sebastian called out as Paul approached. "How's the workout going today?"

Paul tugged his damp T-shirt away from his belly. "Grueling," he answered. "Nobody tells you when you're young how hard it is to stay fit as you get older."

"You're not so old," said Sebastian, with a smile.

"Oh dear boy, bless you," replied Paul, returning the smile. "How is your knee feeling?"

"Better," Sebastian said. "I think that CBD cream you told me about really works. The inflammation has gone down faster, and my muscles feel pretty loose. Thanks for the recommendation."

"Back in my day, we might have just smoked it instead of smearing it on our bodies," said Paul. "But who am I to get in the way of progress?"

Sebastian laughed and stood up from the weight machine. "I

loved those stories you told me about your career in New York City."

"And Los Angeles. So many beautiful people in LA," replied Paul. "Tell me again what kind of work you do."

Sebastian colored. "Well, right now, kind of nothing," he replied, ducking his head. "I just haven't found anything that really interests me, you know, the way fashion did for you."

Paul felt a note of sympathy for Sebastian. "You're smart and curious," he said firmly. "You'll find something soon."

Sebastian held out his fist and tapped it against Paul's. "Thanks, Paul. I really hope so."

"Too bad I'm not still working," Paul said. "We were always looking for fit models. And just look at you . . ." He gestured up and down at Sebastian's toned athletic body. "This would have been in very high demand. You probably could have walked the runway."

"I don't know about that . . ."

"Okay, well being honest, you're right. Your thighs are like mine—kind of large." Paul smoothed his hands over his ample legs. "But you could have at least done promo modeling."

"I think I was too busy going to school," said Sebastian.

"And being a college tennis star."

"Yeah, well look where that got me. Maybe I should have been on the runway," Sebastian said with a laugh.

"Hmmm, maybe." Paul chewed on his lip. "Those thighs though . . . definitely promo."

Sebastian chuckled. He moved to a stationary bike, settled onto the seat, and started pedaling. "So, I saw you just talking with the assistant director of racquet sports . . ." he said over his shoulder.

"Oh, Endy?" replied Paul. "She's fantastic and has become a dear friend. I've never met anyone who is more giving and compassionate."

"Not to mention hot," said Sebastian.

"Not to mention it," Paul raised his eyebrows up. "She's single. I could set you two up if you'd like."

"I think I got it," replied Sebastian. He told Paul about their date the previous evening.

"Aha, so that's why she's in la-la land today . . . a blossoming romance."

"I mean, we've only spent a few hours together, but—"

"Sebastian, let me tell you this right here, right now. Endy is a beloved treasure at Whisper Hills. If you hurt her, I will break your other knee. And everyone else here feels the same. If you hurt her, we will make you so miserable that you'll want—"

"Okay! Okay! I get it, Paul, and I don't doubt that you all could and would," said Sebastian, holding up his hands. "But I'm not planning on hurting her, so you have nothing to worry about."

Sebastian felt eyes on him and slowly looked across the gym. Everyone had stopped their running, stretching, and lifting and were staring at Paul and Sebastian.

Beside the bike he was pedaling, Candi stood near the wall of mirrors. She lifted two fingers in a V, then gestured at her eyes before turning them to point at Sebastian. She mouthed, *I'm watching you.*

Still seated in a lotus position, Earlene nodded and cracked her knuckles.

Sebastian felt his face flush. And then, peeking out from behind a massive inflated balance ball, Nora said in her high, reedy voice, "If you hurt Endy, I will mess you up."

11

Still smiling from her exchange with Paul, Endy set her water bottle on the counter and walked behind the pro shop desk. A star-shaped sticky note with Maria's loopy handwriting in fuchsia glitter ink fluttered in a current of cold air wafting from the air-conditioning overhead.

ENDY'S FAVOR PAYMENT OPTIONS
a) dinner at Indian restaurant on Date Palm Dr
b) Thai foot massages on Sunday
c) all-inclusive women's surf and yoga retreat in Morocco

Smiley faces and dotted illustrations of wiffle balls surrounded the message, reminding Endy of the favor Maria had done by covering for her at Picklers. The funny thing about the list of options was that debt or no debt, Endy would happily do any or all of these activities with her oldest, like-a-sister, best friend.

They'd met in college one early December afternoon when a surprise snowstorm had blown in and the temperatures had dropped way below freezing. Endy had just shut the front gate to her rental, a house in the university district that had been converted to a duplex. She pointed her car's key fob toward her ancient Subaru parked on the street just beyond the front lawn, expecting to hear the chirp of the alarm turning off.

Except it didn't.

She aimed the fob at her car and pressed it over and over, finally throwing it down in frustration into the bare dirt where she'd previously planted petunias and marigolds during the warm months. "Dammit!" she huffed.

"Better pick those keys up before they get buried in snow," came a voice behind her. "Or else you might not find them until spring thaw."

Endy turned around and saw a curvy girl sitting on the stoop of the other half of the duplex. With no roof or overhang for protection from the elements, her arms were wrapped tightly around her voluptuous chest, and she shivered as the snowflakes settled on her mane of thick, curly black hair.

"Sometimes I really hate it here," the girl continued. "And when I say 'sometimes,' I really mean all the time between November and April." She pulled the sleeves of her lightweight sweater over her hands. "Ugh, it's my own damn fault I'm here. I'm still kicking myself."

Endy raised her eyebrows. "For . . . ?"

"For applying to the wrong college," the girl said with a sigh. She gave a feeble wave. "I'm Maria."

"I'm Endy," replied Endy, her head tilted. "Why do you say, 'the wrong college'?"

"Well, I'm from a huge family in LA, and when I was applying to colleges, my cousin's cousin said I should go to school in Florida since we have a lot of family there too. I was so sure I would go to college there that I only applied to the one school, the University of Miami," said Maria. Her lips pursed and she blinked slowly. "U of M."

"But this is U of M . . . the University of Montana," said Endy. And then she burst out laughing. "Oh my god, did you accidentally apply to Montana instead of Miami?"

"And that is why I am still kicking myself." Maria nodded, rolling her eyes. "At least this school gave me a lot of scholarships for my four years. They should have thrown in a down parka as well."

Endy looked over at Maria, noticing that she wasn't even wearing a coat. "So wait, why are you sitting out here on the steps in just a sweater? Are you waiting for someone?"

"No, *soy estúpida*. I'm stupid," Maria sighed. "I locked myself out. My phone is inside, and my roommate doesn't come back from class for forty-five minutes."

"Whoa," said Endy. "You can't stay out here in the storm. Let's go into my place since it looks like I'm not going anywhere with a dead key fob."

"Thanks, that's super nice of you," replied Maria as she stood up and brushed the snow off her arms and hair. "Maybe the storm will get worse and classes will be canceled. We can stay on the couch and drink hot chocolate and tequila."

"That does sound pretty good right now." Endy chuckled and crossed her fingers.

Maria crossed her fingers too, then said, "Anything can happen..."

Endy nodded. "Anything can happen."

The snowstorm did turn into a blizzard. Campus and most of the town shut down. Classes were canceled for the rest of the week, and Endy and Maria became best friends.

Two years later, just days after graduation, Maria had determined that they were going to leave the freezing cold state with "probably the worst Mexican food ever" and move to Mexico City. Maria had family that owned an Airbnb rental property there, and they needed someone to manage it.

Endy, who had never been out of the country before, was reluctant.

"What if I don't like it?" she'd asked Maria as they cleaned their apartment, getting it ready for move out. White trash bags were piled next to the door and dust bunnies coated the floor.

"Oh, *chica*," Maria said as she reached out to hug Endy, her wet rubber gloves dripping down her wrists. "You won't like Mexico City—you'll love it. Everyone does."

"I don't know," replied Endy, resting her head on Maria's shoulder. "It just seems so unpredictable, so random. What if we..."

"Yeah? What if we what?"

"What if we had, like, a plan for the next couple of years? Then we'd know how long we'd be there and when we'd be back."

Maria's big eyes brightened. "*Qué buena*! That's good! My cousin would like to sell the property in a couple of years, so we could come back or do something else when he sells."

Endy smiled. "Two years, in and out."

"Two years, in and out." Maria brushed her rubber-gloved hands together.

So, with a brand-new passport, a fairly new laptop computer, $950 in her checking account, and a roller bag, Endy headed to Mexico City with Maria to start their two-year adventure.

Those couple of years, when Endy and Maria lived in Mexico City, had been the perfect beginning of them being on their own. Mexico City was wonderful, with an insane amount of really good, really affordable restaurants and all the art museums Endy could explore on her time off. They'd both worked for Maria's cousin and shared an apartment in the building at a fraction of what it would have normally cost.

Everything about Mexico City had enchanted Endy. The smells coming from the street vendor's cooking, the constant chatter of a language she didn't understand, the summer downpours that flooded the streets for an hour at a time.

So when Maria's cousin sold the rental property and Endy and Maria were at the end of their two-year stay, they decided to go on another two-year adventure somewhere new.

They found their way to San Francisco, where Maria had a *tia*, an aunty, who had a mother-in-law's apartment in the Mission District they could rent for a couple of years. The apartment had access stairs leading to the roof, and when Maria realized that the door's lock and emergency alarm weren't functioning, she and Endy would often spend their evenings talking and stargazing, laying there on beanbag chairs they'd dragged up.

Endy got a job at the front desk at San Francisco Parks & Rec and took advantage of the free membership and classes for employees. She took a class in a cardio dance-fitness program called BollyX, and a beginner knitting class where she made a charming potholder. But her favorite class of all time was learning how to play pickleball.

Who could have known that Endy would have fallen so in love with pickleball? But it was addictive, and Endy careened fully into it, playing as much as time allowed. She would drive Maria crazy with the flat *tok*, *tok*, *tok*, *tok* sound the ball would make bouncing off her paddle as she walked from room to room in the apartment. So when her supervisors at Parks & Rec realized how obsessed Endy was, they moved her off the front desk and into instructing pickleball.

Pickleball was not her only love. There was also Bennett.

A girl Endy taught in her pickleball class introduced them, and Endy had fallen hard and fast for Bennett. He was more than ready to get into another serious relationship after his previous girlfriend had broken up with him a few months prior. So, within a couple of weeks, Endy and Bennett had gone from dating to spending just about every day with each other. And then it was only two more weeks until they got engaged.

Endy couldn't believe her luck in meeting Bennett. He was good-looking, cultured, well educated, and came from a wealthy family in Seattle, so Endy did everything she could to be the type of woman he would want to spend his life with.

Endy slowly adopted Bennett's mannerisms and chose to become quiet and respectful of his opinions. She knew Maria didn't approve of the changes to her personality, but Endy had had unsuccessful relationships before in her life, and she did everything she could to make sure this relationship was the one that would succeed.

But when Bennett's ex-girlfriend arrived back in San Francisco after living in Barcelona for the past few years, she had run right back to him, begging his forgiveness and telling him how much she had missed him. Immediately, it was glaringly clear how well suited they were for each other, much more so than Endy had ever been in Bennett's world. And within a month, Bennett left Endy to get back together with his ex, and Endy found herself heartbroken and un-engaged.

Maria and Endy sat on their apartment's rooftop, eating ice cream out of the containers.

"I am so sorry about the bad news from my *tia*," said Maria, licking her spoon. "I can't believe she's raising the rent on our place."

"It's not your aunty's fault," replied Endy. "She gave us a pretty sweet deal these past couple of years. There's no chance we can afford to stay any longer."

Endy placed the container of ice cream next to her, then lay back. Darkness pressed heavy on the rooftop, and Endy felt Maria recline next to her.

"It's time, anyway," Endy said in a low voice. "Now that Bennett and I aren't together, nothing is keeping me here. I think a change of scene is probably a good idea."

"I hate that you had to go through that with Bennett," said Maria, reaching out and wrapping her fingers in Endy's. "But, *amiga*, he wasn't the one. You deserve better."

"Better?" argued Endy. "You know who was better? She was. Prettier, smarter, richer."

"Shut your mouth!" replied Maria. "The next guy who falls in love with you is going to be the one."

"Sure, until his beautiful ex-girlfriend comes back. Just like—" Endy said. "Ouch! Did you just pinch me?"

Maria sat up. "And I'll do it again every time you say you're not good enough for some guy. Plus, the probability of an ex coming back and stealing your boyfriend away from you again is, like, one in a million."

"Okay, okay, I get it." Endy sighed. "Maybe your aunt raising our rent is a sign. I need a change, which means you do too, bestie."

"We go together," Maria nodded. "But aren't you worried about what we're going to do next?"

"Kind of," replied Endy. "But it'll work—"

"Oh my god, did you see it? Another sign!" exclaimed Maria, as a streak of light crossed the night sky. "Make a wish!"

Already ahead of Maria, Endy squeezed her eyes closed and crossed her fingers. "Please come true," she whispered, her wish on the shooting star serious and weighty in her heart. *"Please."*

When she'd arrived home from work the next day, she'd barely stepped through the door when Maria came rushing toward her, breathless.

"Just what did you wish for when we saw the shooting star?"

"What did I wish for? Why?" asked Endy with a blank look.

"Because . . . pack your sunscreen," Maria yelled, jumping up and down. "We're going to sunny SoCal!"

"Wait, what?"

Maria grabbed Endy's arms, a smile wide across her face. "We are moving to Palm Springs! My cousin got us jobs at a country club called Whisper Hills!"

Endy's eyes widened and she enveloped Maria in a hug. "What just happened?"

"That wishing on a shooting star thing really worked, because they want us down there in two weeks."

So with a brand-new tube of SPF 50-plus sunblock, a fairly new two-piece swimsuit, $700 in her checking account, and a roller bag, Endy headed to Palm Springs with her best friend, starting another two-year adventure.

Endy fished a black Sharpie from the messy desk drawer under the pro shop's computer and wrote in between the lines and smiley faces.

ENDY'S FAVOR PAYMENT OPTIONS
a) dinner at Indian restaurant on Date Palm Dr
**my treat this Saturday. But you are NOT allowed to order spicy level 6 EVER AGAIN
b) Thai foot massages on Sunday
**yaasss, s/b every Sunday for our whole lives
c) all-inclusive women's surf and yoga retreat in Morocco
**in 2 years???

She placed the sticky note on the frame of the computer screen and smoothed it with her thumb, smiling at her great fortune to have people like Paul Rothman and Maria Gutierrez in her life.

12

When she arrived home, the window curtains in her casita were drawn against the daytime heat and the thick mustard-colored walls topped by terra-cotta roof tiles radiated warmth. The yard was choked in spikey bougainvillea vines, and the path to her front door was smothered in papery magenta blooms and desert sand. A neighbor's pit bull barked a welcome from behind the fence, but in the nighttime darkness, all else was quiet.

Endy stopped on the pathway and smiled at Maria perched on the front step, illuminated by the overhead porch light. "Hey, what are you doing here?"

"I brought ice cream," she said, holding up an insulated tote.

"Uh-oh. What's wrong?"

"Why does something have to be wrong? Can't I come over to my bestie's house just to hang out with her?"

"Well, yeah," replied Endy, "but you brought ice cream. So something's wrong."

"There's nothing wrong." Maria stood up and brushed at the seat of her black yoga pants. "I get the salted caramel first."

Endy pushed open her door and clicked on a lamp. A lone green sofa with lumpy pillows and sunken cushions and an oak-laminate dining set with four chairs took up most of the front room. The walls and floor were bare, and the built-in shelves lining the living room wall were empty. There was no television, no plants, no pictures.

Endy kicked off her shoes and went into the kitchen. She opened a drawer and selected two spoons from the five she owned, then plopped down on the sofa next to Maria.

Maria pried the lid off the container and stuck her spoon in immediately. "So, I've been thinking . . ."

"Is this where you tell me nothing's wrong?"

"Nothing is wrong, Endy," replied Maria, exasperated. "I've just been thinking that we've been here, in Palm Springs, for almost two years and I kind of like it more than I thought I would."

Endy nodded and dug her spoon into the pint of chocolate chip cookie dough. "Me too."

"Valid, right?"

"Yep."

"So then, do you think we're going to stay here for a while?" asked Maria, her head tilted. "I mean, this would be the first time we'd live someplace for more than two years."

Endy took another bite of ice cream. "That would be great by me, but I'll need to find a new place to live since my landlords are planning to sell this casita at the end of the season. And I want to make sure that Picklers gets funded for the next couple of years."

"¡*Ay!*" moaned Maria, rubbing at her temples. She breathed out. "Brain freeze."

"Ouch, I hate those," agreed Endy. She waited until Maria had stopped grimacing, then asked, "So, how do you feel about us staying?"

Maria slowly licked her spoon and then dipped it into the pint Endy held. "Well . . ."

"Okay, this is where you tell me something's wrong."

"Nothing is wrong! I just was thinking that if we decide to stay here for a while, it might be nice to meet some other people. You know, make more friends."

Endy slid a glance at Maria. "After eight years, are you finally getting sick of me?"

"No, never! You'll always be my bestie, Endy. But I worry that if something happens to one of us, the other will be left . . . alone."

"What could possibly happen to one of us?"

"I don't know. I'm just saying that I want us to find more friends who don't work at the pro shop or who are, like, either ten or seventy years old."

Endy chuckled. Maria was right. They didn't really have any friends their age. And spending their days working at the racquet pro shop or with Picklers hadn't helped that. The idea of staying in Palm Springs was appealing to Endy, so if they were going to break their two-year pattern, then they really should find more friends.

"Okay, I agree, it's a good idea," Endy replied as she dipped her spoon in her carton and scooped out the last bite. "Let's make new friends."

13

The next afternoon, after they'd worked hard to restock the shop, sweep off the patio, and arrange match play, Endy and Maria stood at the front desk looking over the next day's schedule. Joel walked past them holding a tennis racquet. He stopped and turned back to Endy and looked at her from beneath his eyebrows.

"Sebastian Hall and I are going to the Stout House this Friday," he said. "He wanted me to invite you guys to meet up with us."

"Did he?" Endy smiled.

"Yeah," replied Joel. He studied Endy. "I didn't know you knew him."

"I don't, really. I mean, we had some wine and talked . . ."

". . . the other night," finished Joel.

Endy's eyes narrowed, and she frowned. "How do you know about the other night?"

"I saw you get into his golf cart after you got off work. Seems to me that you guys were pretty chummy."

"Seems to me that it's none of your business." Endy again had the sense that Joel was jealous, which kind of baffled her. They had dated briefly when she had first moved to Palm Springs. He was certainly more than attractive enough in that jock-ish way with hair that is messy but not too messy, strong shoulders, and six-pack abs. Joel was confident and cocky, so girls were drawn to him, and he never went long without some girlfriend pining over him.

Endy and Joel were super comfortable around each other. While workplace romances tended to happen everywhere, Endy hadn't felt a special spark with him, so their relationship was over within a few months. She had broken it off, telling him that it was uncomfortable for her to be dating someone who was her boss.

Joel hadn't wanted to call it off, but Endy said she wanted to keep things professional, so he'd reluctantly agreed. Very reluctantly.

She thought about Joel's earlier behavior when she'd brought Sebastian the ice for his twisted knee. Was Joel jealous? And is that why he had shoved himself between her and Sebastian when she'd tried to help him to the bench? But the idea of Joel being jealous was ridiculous . . . Endy barely knew Sebastian.

Except, when Endy had brought Sebastian to his car, she'd noticed a blue and gold bumper sticker with a brown bear—a UCLA bruin. Sebastian had mentioned that he knew Joel from when they played college tennis. And Endy knew that Joel had gone to the University of Southern California. In fact, pretty much everyone knew Joel had gone to USC since his saying of choice was a smug "Fight on."

From what Endy had seen over the past few days, just like their college rivalry, Sebastian and Joel were well matched . . . and extremely competitive.

Joel was quiet as he walked to the stringing machine and placed the tennis racquet on top. Finally, with a surly glance at Endy, he said, "You know, Sebastian is messed up."

Endy returned his glance. "Yeah, he said something about how he keeps reinjuring his knee."

"Not like that, Endy," said Joel. "Well, yeah, that too, sure. But what I mean is that he has a reputation as being a quitter."

Endy's eyebrows drew together, and she looked at Maria, who just shrugged.

"When we played against each other, Sebastian was literally the best in Pac-12 tennis," continued Joel. "His college career was the stuff of legends. When he played for UCLA, he helped them win three straight NCAA Team Championships, and hell, he himself won a couple of NCAA Singles Championships."

Maria moved from behind the front counter. "Doesn't sound messed up to me."

"It's what happened after all that. Everyone thought that Sebastian would turn professional. *Everyone* said it—he was that good. But during one match, I think it was at the end of his junior year, he was playing against Ivan Kovacic—"

"Wait, the Ivan Kovacic who just made it to the quarter-finals at the US Open?" asked Maria, her eyebrows raised. Joel nodded.

"So Sebastian was actually winning against Kovacic. He had won the first set pretty convincingly but was down a break in the second set." Joel leaned his arms against the stringing machine. "Kovacic served this bomb out wide, and Sebastian lunged to get to it. But instead, his knee twisted and bent back under him, completely the wrong way." Joel's torso shook as he visibly shivered. "We were all there watching. Even now just remembering it and what it looked like makes me feel like throwing up."

Endy approached Joel, her eyes full of concern. "Okay, but you said he wasn't messed up because of his knee. And yet . . ."

"Right. See, he could have gotten it completely fixed by any of those world-renowned doctors in LA, and he probably could have done rehab and come back to play his senior year." Joel shrugged his shoulders and shook his head. "But he didn't. He just up and quit tennis altogether. So it's no wonder he said he felt like his knee never fully healed. He's a fucking quitter."

"Come on, Joel. Give him a break. Sebastian had his dream of becoming a pro tennis player crushed along with his knee."

"But was it? His dream, I mean." Joel picked up the tennis racquet and started snipping the strings. "After what happened with his knee, Sebastian sure wasn't interested in becoming a pro tennis player any longer. He wasn't interested in tennis, or actually . . . *anything*. Just up and quit everything. And since then, I don't know if he's *ever* found anything he's interested in."

Endy couldn't decide how much of this history to believe. "Have you ever asked him what he—"

"He wasn't even interested in Sloane anymore," interrupted Joel. "Broke off their engagement, which surprised everyone, especially her."

Sebastian was engaged?

"Sebastian hasn't really done anything since he quit tennis, and then quit Sloane." Joel frowned and crossed his arms. "So yeah, I think that makes him both messed up and a quitter."

They all remained quiet for a bit after Joel finished this story. Endy retreated to her office and pretended to go through all the emails on her computer. But her mind was buzzing with thoughts of Sebastian.

A knock at her door pulled Endy out of her thoughts. Maria entered and sat in the chair across from Endy's desk. "What was all that about?" she asked. "Who is this Sebastian that Joel was talking about? And why is he so wildly jealous of him?" Maria looked over her shoulder, then turned back to Endy. "You can talk. He already left for the day."

Endy raised her hand and pinched the bridge of her nose. "Sebastian Hall," she started. "The hottest, most handsome, most incredible . . ."

"Wait, what?" screamed Maria as she leaned close to Endy, a huge grin on her face. "Why didn't you tell me about him when I was at your house last night?"

Endy laughed. "I guess I wasn't even thinking about him because we got so caught up talking about trying to make more friends here."

"He could be a *friend*." Maria lifted her hands, and her fingers made quotes in the air. "What is even going on? Spill everything!"

Over the next half hour, Endy recounted everything—from how she'd run into Sebastian when she was late to Picklers, to bringing him ice, to laughing uncontrollably with him on the golf cart. By the time Endy got to the part where she and Sebastian had shared a bottle of wine a couple of evenings before, Maria was whooping and dancing around Endy's office.

"I dunno, don't read anything into this. He might just be like this with everyone, you know, super nice, kinda flirty . . ."

"I've never seen Joel act like he did today. He knows there is something up between you and Sebastian."

"There is nothing *up* between me and Sebastian Hall."

"I'll be the judge of that," replied Maria, still doing little hip shakes. "But I'm going home now. I gotta light some kind of candles and put out some prayer flags or *something* for you. You've found our first new friend, Endy." She winked.

"Maria, please, please don't make this into something it's not." Endy dropped her face into her palms.

Maria smiled at Endy, leaned across the desk, and planted a kiss on her head. She backed out of the office, holding both hands up with fingers crossed, and a wicked grin playing across her red lips.

14

Endy and Maria walked into the Stout House, a busy sports bar with fifty-one different beers on tap and dozens of screens mounted above the bar, each showing a different sport. They stopped just inside the door, letting their eyes adjust to the dimness. The Friday evening crowd packed in, with every table full and people standing two or three deep at the bar.

"There they are," Maria said, standing on a step. She tugged on Endy's sleeve, and they made their way to the booth in the back corner where Joel, Sebastian, and Collin Park sat.

"Hey guys," greeted Maria as she slid in next to Collin.

Endy took the open seat next to Joel, then leaned past him. "Sebastian, this is my friend Maria."

Sebastian reached across the table to shake Maria's hand, the muscles in his arms rippling. With a wicked grin, Maria shook his hand and kicked Endy under the table.

"Ow!" Endy exclaimed, clapping a hand across her mouth.

A waitress arrived and set down two glasses of white wine, one in front of Maria, the other in front of Endy, then rushed away to tend to the booth next to them. Endy raised her eyebrows. "We haven't ord—"

"I hope it's okay that I put in an order for you guys," said Sebastian. "It's so busy in here that it's been hard to get our server's attention. And I didn't want you to have to wait."

Endy and Maria looked at each other and smiled. Maria took a sip of the chilled wine and said, "Oh, this is nice."

Sebastian nodded and looked at Endy. "It's the same wine we had the other night."

Endy took a sip. "Very thoughtful of you, Sebastian." She slid a glance at Joel, whose eyes were slightly darkened, and he was chewing the inside of his cheek.

A TV monitor on the opposite wall played highlights of the recent Australian Open tennis tournament. Watching the last point, Collin lifted his arms from under the table and pumped them in the air. "Oh my god, that shot was incredible," he said.

Maria stared at Collin's raised arms. Bandages wrapped him from the tips of his fingers to his elbows.

"Dude," she exclaimed. "What in the hell happened to you?"

Collin clasped his pint glass with both of his wrapped hands and took a long sip of beer. "I was playing pickleball with my cousins and went running for the ball that they hit over the fence." A roaring cheer came from across the bar where a sizable crowd was watching a live golf tournament being played.

Endy winced. "And that happened when you fell on the court?"

"No." Collin rolled his eyes. "Actually, I tripped when I reached for the ball and fell into a bunch of cacti."

"*¡Ayyy!*" Maria's hands flew to her mouth. "One time I stepped on a pile of bougainvillea trimmings, and a two-inch thorn nailed my flip-flop to my foot."

Collin laughed. "In the summers during college, I worked on a gardening crew to earn money for tuition. Stuff like that happened to us all the time." He and Maria touched their glasses together in a kind of toast.

"I taught kids tennis lessons during my summers," said Joel, sipping his beer. "Wasn't cheap going to USC."

Sebastian gave a wry smile and said, "Fight on, Joel."

"Fuck you, Sebastian," snapped Joel. "The only person at this table who didn't have to help pay their own way through college is you. You've never had to pay for anything for yourself." Joel downed the last of the beer in his glass. "You don't even have a job right now."

The table went quiet at Joel's rant. Endy looked from Joel to Sebastian, then shot her arm up, signaling to their waitress to bring another round of drinks.

Sebastian twirled his empty glass in his hands. "You know that I had a full-ride tennis scholarship at UCLA," he said quietly. "And now I live off the interest from my investments. I haven't taken money from my parents since I was a kid."

"Maybe not, but the rest of us at this table probably aren't in line for their family inheritance," scoffed Joel. He pushed away his empty glass without meeting Sebastian's gaze.

Sebastian shot Joel an irritated glance. "What is this? Some kind of competition, like a weird trust fund contest?"

"No. But even if it were and you won, it'd only be by default."

Sebastian rolled his eyes and leaned back in his seat.

An uncomfortable silence descended on the booth, and each of them pretended to watch a game playing on the overhead televisions. Endy gnawed at her thumbnail, and Maria pulled out her phone and started scrolling.

The waitress arrived and placed a tray full of drinks on the table. "Everyone doing okay?" she asked.

"We are now," replied Endy as she pushed a full glass of beer toward Joel. She looked around the table. "Anybody want to share a pizza?"

They put in their order for pizza, and then Endy and Maria excused themselves to go to the restroom.

Sitting in the stall next to Endy, Maria said, "Man, Joel really went there with Sebastian."

"I know," agreed Endy. "I mean, sometimes Joel can be a jerk, but I've never really seen him go after somebody like that."

They both flushed and opened the stall doors at the same time. Grinning at each other, they went to wash their hands and studied their reflections in the mirror.

"That's what I'm saying, Endy," said Maria, fluffing up her glossy curls. "Joel still has a thing for you. He's super jealous."

"Joel has nothing to be jealous about," Endy responded.

"*That's very thoughtful of you, Sebastian,*" Maria said in a breathy voice. "*Are you always so thoughtful, Sebastian? Like in bed, Sebastian?*"

Endy burst out laughing and shoved Maria away from the sinks. She pulled open the restroom door and stepped out. "Two glasses of wine and you turn into a comic."

Maria pulled Endy into a hug and kissed her cheek. "I'm funny when I drink wine. You don't want to hear me when I drink tequila."

Endy returned Maria's hug. "Oh, believe me, I know . . . *I know.*"

Two stunning waitresses were at their table, obviously capturing Joel's and Collin's attention. All four of them, having fun flirting. Across the restaurant, the dozens of televisions blasted coverage of different sports, interrupted only by ads. Bartenders moved behind the bar, pulling yards of draft beer and salting rims of margarita glasses.

Sebastian limped up behind Endy and placed his hand on the small of her back.

He leaned in, his mouth near her ear. "I could hear you two screaming with laughter while I was in the men's room."

"You couldn't!" Endy felt her face getting hot and turning red. "What did you hear?" She pinched the bridge of her nose, trying to play it cool, and slid into the booth next to Joel. Maria took her seat next to Collin, and Sebastian slid in next to Endy.

He leaned in again and whispered, "Nothing." He chuckled. "I didn't hear anything except you girls cackling."

"Thank god," replied Endy, blowing out a deep breath, and shaking her head.

A slow grin played across Sebastian's lips. "But now I definitely need to know what you were talking about."

15

Endy stood between the courts watching the kids, while a loud, persistent honking blared from a car alarm in the nearby parking lot. Her shoulders felt tense, and she gnawed at her thumbnail.

She had spent the last hour of her workday going over the budget needed to keep Picklers going for another two years. The fundraising event was in a couple of weeks, and hundreds of invitations had already been sent out for the charity pickleball tournament that Endy had named the Paddle Battle. They were matching kids from the program with adults from Whisper Hills, as well as from throughout the Coachella Valley, who would buy onto the doubles team. But even with donations from a dozen local businesses, they still weren't even close to the $25,000 the program needed. They desperately needed more sign-ups.

As director of racquet sports, Joel was already signed up to play. He would get to pick his junior partner, and Endy felt certain Joel would choose one of the more athletic boys. He had told Endy that he'd be by the Picklers' practice that day to scout for his perfect junior partner.

The practice was well attended, with all fifteen courts filled with four kids each. Endy had grouped the kids by age more than by ability for practice but would be sensitive to pairing partners during the Paddle Battle so that play would be equal during the competition. That way, hopefully, everyone would have fun, and donors would reach deeper into their wallets.

She scanned the full courts when she heard the fight break out.

"You didn't have to hit me in the face!"

"I didn't do it on purpose. You walked into my shot."

"No, I didn't!"

"Yeah, man, you did. But look, I'm sorry you got hit with the ball. It didn't hurt that much, right?"

The boy glared at Paco and turned away to walk back to the baseline. Still at the net, Paco tossed the bright green plastic ball up and swiped at it with his paddle, sending the ball into the retreating kid's back, right in the middle of the large zero printed on the back of his Celtics jersey. A devilish grin spread across Paco's face.

"Who's the little hothead?" asked Joel, coming up behind Endy.

"Paco Lopez," replied Endy, chewing at the inside of her cheek. "He's kind of uncontrollable . . . but really, he is crazy talented."

"More like plain old crazy, if you ask me," Joel replied. He looked over the courts, his arms crossed and lips pursed, occasionally nodding. The players on the court closest to them played cautiously, methodically trading shots. *Dinka, dinka, dinka, dinka . . . dinka . . . dinka . . . dinka.*

Joel made a gagging noise. "Are we going to be here all night until somebody actually makes a point?"

Endy shot him a glance, then rolled her eyes. "Just choose a partner, Joel."

He looked to the middle court where Paco was hitting the pickleball into the fence repeatedly as his partners stood at the net with frowns plastered on their faces. Joel shook his head. "Yeah, no," he said. "Hard pass."

Endy sighed.

But then, Joel pointed to the farthest court at a tall athletic boy moving with sure, quick movements. "Who's that?"

"Brayden Sato. His mom works over in admin at the clubhouse."

"He's good. How old?"

"Sixteen, seventeen sometime this spring."

They watched points being played, with Brayden serving, then moving forward and hitting a smooth shot over the net. He stayed bent at his knees, his paddle up so when the ball came back to him, he returned it in a fluid move of his arm and wrist. Brayden was clearly the most competent player of all sixty kids across the filled courts.

"I want him," said Joel. He snapped his fingers then put his index finger and thumb out and pointed at Brayden. "That's my partner."

"Of course he is," replied Endy, drawing a number one next to Brayden's name, and then again next to Joel's. "You know, Joel, remember that the Paddle Battle is a fundraiser. We should be playing for fun."

"It's called Paddle *Battle*," replied Joel. "I play to win."

Endy groaned. She turned from Joel just as an incredibly handsome, fit brunet gingerly walked toward them. A smile played at her lips—she couldn't help herself.

"What are you doing here?" asked Joel, crossing his arms over his chest, obviously annoyed. The car alarm continued blaring in the distance.

Sebastian held up his hand in a small wave. "I just left physical therapy at the sports club and was driving by. Saw you two and thought I'd come see if I could help out with whatever you're doing here."

Joel plastered a smile on his face and stepped closer to Endy. "Endy and I have things handled."

A shout came from the middle pickleball court. "Paco, stop it!"

They looked over to where Paco, his mouth full, spun in a circle spewing water like a sprinkler head.

"PAAAACCCCOOOO, stop!"

Sebastian looked from Joel to Endy, a corner of his mouth lifted. "Yep, sure looks like everything's handled here."

A whistle came from a car that had just rolled to a stop next to the courts. Through the open window, a woman shouted, *"Jorge! Estoy aquí!"*

"Sorry, Endy, but I have to leave. We gotta go visit my grandma in the hospital." A young boy ran past, grabbing a backpack off the table on his way to the parked car.

Endy, Joel, and Sebastian stood rooted. "Um, okay . . ." Endy mumbled. "Wha—"

"They need another player!" came a shout from the middle court. Endy looked over and saw a player waving his hands above his head. Next to the boy, Paco hit the pickleball at the feet of the two girls waiting next to him, their threesome now missing a fourth.

"Paco, stop!" one of them yelled. But Paco ignored the plea and kept pestering the girls, who continued to yell.

Joel jerked his head, his eyebrows drawn together. "Do something about that, will you?" he said to Endy, running his hand through his hair. "I chose my partner, and now I'm outta here."

Joel headed for the far court, his eyes focused on Brayden, his steps brisk. Endy glanced around at the other courts, then quickly followed behind Joel.

"Joel, hold up," she called. "Wait for me so I can introduce you guys."

After making sure Joel and Brayden had met, and explaining how the fundraiser would work, Endy hurried back to the other kids. By the time her attention returned to them, she saw that Sebastian had made his way onto the middle pickleball court and was holding a paddle.

He towered over Paco, and both wore looks of concentration. Paco gestured with his paddle at the net, then the baseline, then pointed at the ground and Endy heard him say, "Just stay out of the kitchen."

"What's the kitchen?"

"Just do what I say," replied Paco, slapping a palm on his forehead.

"Alright, I guess I'm ready to play," said Sebastian, nodding. He looked at the girls on the other side of the net.

"Okay," Paco replied. "Let's do it, losers."

Sebastian was on the court with the three kids for the rest of their practice. Being careful of his injured knee, he barely moved from his position, but because of his long arms and obvious comfort with a racquet in his hand, he barely had to. Although he was a quick study, the girls won convincingly, and they skipped off the court with their ponytails swinging and big smiles across their faces.

Paco was obviously disgruntled, but he walked off the court beside Sebastian, both gripping their pickleball paddles tightly.

Endy corralled the kids at the end of practice, making sure they had their belongings, and then she collected all the pickleball gear left on the table and strewn across the grass. Evening was coming on fast, and the country club had turned quiet. Traffic from outside the club kept up a constant murmur, with the occasional deep thrum of a semitruck's air brakes, the sound deep and low.

As most of the kids were being picked up, Paco leaned against the fence, his leg jiggling, waiting again for his mother. Sebastian approached him, carrying two paddles, and Endy saw them walk back onto the pickleball court.

Sebastian went to one side of the net, Paco to the opposite. Sebastian hit the first ball over, then Paco returned it. They hit the ball smoothly back and forth, with Endy counting the number of hits. Fifty-four before the ball finally hit the net, putting an end to their rally.

Endy heard a car door slam, and she saw Valentina crossing the grass toward her.

"Endy, thank you so much for always waiting for me to get here," said Valentina, her hand on Endy's arm. "I'm the Mexican mom who is always 'almost there' when I'm nowhere close to being 'almost there.'" Valentina started laughing.

Endy grinned. "Well, I got up early this morning so I could be late for work without rushing." She put her hands on her hips.

Valentina's eyes crinkled. "We wake up late, and we're late. We wake up early, and we're . . ."

". . . also late," they said in unison, laughing so hard that they had to lean against each other.

"Girl," said Valentina, wiping tears from her eyes. "We are so lucky. Promise that you'll stay with us until Paco finishes high school. What would all of us do without you?" She put her arms around Endy and squeezed.

"Jeez, Mom, why do you always gotta be so huggy?" said Paco as he jogged up to them. "Let's go." He grabbed Valentina's jacket sleeve and dragged her toward the car. Walking away, Valentina put her arm around her son's shoulders and turned back to give Endy a wink.

Endy smiled as she watched them walk to the car. Then she turned to the mess remaining under the awning.

There, Sebastian sat on a tabletop, his feet resting on the bench seat. His hairline was damp, and he pulled the hem of his T-shirt up to wipe the sweat from his face. Endy glanced at his flat, well-defined muscles peeking out from the bottom of his shirt. She inhaled deeply, smelling his delicious scent, a citrusy and earthy masculine combination. Sebastian really was dreamy, and Endy's body responded, leaving her a bit lightheaded.

Sebastian noticed her faltering, so he shifted on the table and patted next to him, the gesture both friendly and seductive.

He handed her a bottle of water as she settled in beside him. "I'm glad you're wearing that cute little skirt," he said, looking her up and down out of the side of his eyes. Endy felt her face getting warm, and she smoothed the lavender-colored tennis skirt across her thighs. "You had that on when we first ran into each other. But then, you also had on a T-shirt that said 'big dink energy.'"

Endy laughed. "I can't believe you remember that. Sorry again for running off that day. I was late—"

"You don't like being late," Sebastian commented with a grin. "But you're so *good* at it."

Endy chuckled. "You overheard Valentina and me."

"Yeah. It seems like she really likes you," Sebastian said as he turned to fully face Endy. "All the people here seem to really like you." A breeze blew across the table, and Sebastian tucked a loose strand of Endy's hair behind her ear.

Endy smiled. "I like them, too."

"I kind of really like you," said Sebastian, a slow grin playing on his lips. His gaze covered Endy's face, and over the hum of the desert slowing for the evening, they stared at each other with shallow breaths.

Endy looked down and bit her lower lip. Sebastian's hand reached out and . . . *Clunk!* A hard bright green plastic ball flew through the air, hitting and bouncing off Endy's head.

"He likes you!" Paco called out, making kissing noises as he ran up to the table. "Forgot something!"

He grabbed his backpack from underneath them and ran back to his mom's car.

16

Endy drove slowly around the perimeter of the racquet club, the golf cart making an occasional scraping noise as she rolled over the speed bumps in the road. Picklers weren't scheduled for practice, so she could take her time and enjoy the end of the day. The air smelled of heat, and the club was quiet, with most people settling down to their first cocktail of the evening.

In the quiet of the approaching dusk, the noise coming from the two pickleball courts at the far end of the racquet club sounded raucous, with the usual music and loud whoops filling the air.

Endy smiled to herself as the golf cart rounded the farthest point of the property and the pro shop came into view over the manicured grass of the croquet courts. The LED lights mounted on the tall poles over the sports courts had not yet blinked on, but night was just minutes away. The paths in between the courts were deserted with the exception of an elegantly dressed, older woman holding the leash to a black-and-white cocker spaniel that had stopped to sniff at the base of a nearby bougainvillea bush.

A loud cheer came from the pickleball courts causing the dog to startle. He pulled his leash from the woman's hand, then darted off.

"Ollie, come back this instant! Ollie!"

From the safety beneath the bougainvillea bushes, a black-and-white tail trembled. The woman clicked her tongue, and a muscle in her jaw twitched as she knelt to pick up the leash that had dragged across the path.

Endy slowed the cart and rolled to a stop. "Good evening, Mrs. Tennyson." Endy remembered their last interaction, just a few days ago during the community meeting, when Barbara had given her an icy stare and questioned whether a full-time employee was needed to run the pickleball program.

The attractive older woman glanced up. "The same to you, Miss . . ."

"Andrews. Endy Andrews, from the racquet club pro shop."

"Ah yes," replied Barbara Tennyson. "The pickleball girl."

Endy reddened and tucked a strand of hair behind her ear. "Well, I'm not *just* the—"

Another boisterous roar erupted from the pickleball courts, the players screaming and laughing.

Barbara's lips pursed. "No, no . . . you are," she said softly over her shoulder as she turned her back to Endy and, pulling at the dog's leash, stepped away.

17

Moths dipped and dodged in the glaring overhead LED lights. All twenty of the pickleball courts were full, and loud cheers blended with the *thwack* of hard paddles on plastic wiffle balls. Taylor Swift blasted from the speaker on one of the picnic tables under the awning littered with plastic water bottles and empty beer and hard seltzer cans.

"Thanks for putting on this event." Dr. Markowitz sat in a folding chair, his leg elevated on a red Igloo cooler. "I've missed this crazy group."

"They've all missed you too," Endy spoke loudly, over the din. "How are you healing up?"

"Too slowly, if you ask me. But that is typical for Achilles tendon tears on us old folks."

Endy put her hand on Steven's shoulder and squeezed.

"Rumor has it that some of the club members are trying to get pickleball shut down," Steven said, sipping from an insulated pint glass, the ice cubes clinking inside.

"Yeah, it seems that with pickleball, people either love it or hate it. But what I don't understand is why the haters hate it so much that they want to get rid of it." On the courts in front of them, players stepped in and out, taking their turns at play.

Steven answered loudly. "It's the tennis purists. All those original homeowners who bought property here because Whisper Hills was the premier tennis club in the desert." He sipped his drink. "They all rubbed shoulders with the likes of Jimmy Connors and Boris Becker when they'd come over here and practice. And then afterward, the homeowners would host the pros at these swanky poolside parties in their homes. Everyone had a crystal champagne glass in their hand and a Dunlop tennis bag in their hall closet."

Endy sighed. Tennis purists—it made sense. And it was worrisome. What about her job? Endy had put in a ton of work over the past couple of years, building the pickleball community inside the club. Although her title was assistant director of racquet sports, Endy didn't really have much experience on the tennis side of things. She managed and oversaw programs in pickleball and, yes, tennis, but really, Joel was the tennis pro and did all the instruction. If the pickleball program was scrubbed at Whisper Hills, would her position even be necessary any longer? Would she be let go?

Steven swirled the ice cubes in his cup and then gestured in the vicinity of a large Spanish-style house across the street. Endy looked beyond to a heavy, ornate wrought iron gate flanked by bright white stucco walls and a roof topped by terra-cotta tiles. A manicured desert garden of succulents and agaves surrounded a bubbling two-tiered fountain under a line of sky-high palm trees. A four-car garage wrapped around the side, with one of the doors smaller, in miniature, for housing a golf cart.

"Speaking of tennis purists, that was the very first property built here," Steven continued. "The Tennysons'."

"Like, as in Barbara Tennyson?" Endy's eyes opened wide.

Hollers filled the air across the pickleball court for another player to come fill an empty position as Paul Rothman limped toward them.

"Dehydrated," was the reply to the unasked question. Paul lifted Steven's leg from the cooler and pulled out a dripping Gatorade, cracked the lid off, and guzzled.

"Did I hear you two talking about the Tennysons?" Paul asked, as he dug a towel out from his bag, then mopped at his forehead and face.

Endy nodded as she handed Paul a banana. "You need potassium."

"Yeah, Barbara and her husband, Clive, were among the original Whisper Hills Country Club members," Paul continued. "Clive was a top 25 player in his day—professional from England. Barbara traveled to all his tournaments with him for years, but then he retired and they moved here to raise their kids."

Steven nodded. "None of their kids got the tennis bug, but Clive was out here playing every day and—"

"—and Barbara would sit on that bench over there and watch." Paul pointed with the banana to a carved wood bench overlooking the far pickleball courts, closest to the pro shop building. Endy saw a small bronze plaque affixed to the bench back, winking in the overhead lights. "Every match. She watched every single match."

"But you said none of their kids played tennis?" asked Endy.

"No, the Tennyson daughter got married and really wasn't around much," Steven answered with a shrug. "But I guess one of the grandkids picked it up and was supposedly pretty good."

"Huh," replied Endy. "I wonder what ever happened to them."

"Probably living a life of leisure, while we've been working our fingers to the bone," Steven said, pretending to wipe his tears away.

"You were a plastic surgeon." Paul jostled Steven's chair. "And you retired at age forty-nine with plenty of meat on your fingers."

"I didn't retire," sniffed Steven. "I merely cut back my hours."

The dozens of pickleballers continued playing in rotation. During their brief pauses in between matches, they'd gather at the tables under the awning, guzzling water and sipping beer, wine, or hard seltzers. Louder even than the booming music, their joyful laughter echoed across the country club grounds.

George Jacobs held a red plastic cup in the air. "Pickleball is life!" he crowed, which drew whistles and claps from the crowd.

Endy's phone chimed loudly, vibrating in her pocket. She pulled it out and clicked off the alarm. It was ten o'clock and time to shut down the festivities.

Making her way to the picnic table, she turned off the music, which drew a loud protest from the crowd.

"Sorry everyone, the bar's closing!" she yelled out.

"Booooo," replied the pickleballers still on the courts. Yet they put down their paddles and ceased play. They were homeowners as well and knew the HOA rules, so they moved from the courts without fuss, laughing and singing.

The pickleball players gathered crushed cups and cans, empty chip bags and banana peels, and deposited it all into the trash cans at the edge of the courts. An older couple coaxed their small pug from underneath a camp chair. The dog blinked drowsily and wheezed a few times as it got to its feet.

When finally the area was cleared, the last pickleballers headed home in their golf carts or walked away down the middle of the deserted street. Endy surveyed the space. It was clean and ready for another day of play tomorrow. She clicked off the massive overhead lights and darkness wrapped around her.

After such a busy and fun-filled evening, Endy realized that she wasn't quite ready to head home yet. She cracked open a hard seltzer that Steven had left for her, the *hisssss* sharp in the surrounding quiet, and walked to the grass tennis courts. A sliver of moon glowed directly above her, bright stars blinked, and the warm desert breeze lifted strands of her hair.

She sat down in the middle of the grass and sipped at her drink. The evening had been a blast and a wild success. And yet there were those rumors about some people wanting to get rid of the pickleball program entirely. Endy shook her head. Why would anyone want to shut down something that brought so many people joy?

She set the can next to her and stretched out on her back just as a shooting star streaked by overhead. Endy remembered when she'd last seen a shooting star. It was a couple of years ago, on their San Francisco rooftop with Maria. And now look where they were after her wish had actually come true.

Closing her eyes, Endy made another wish, different from the last, but still really, really hoping that this wish might come to fruition too.

Settling into the grass carpet, Endy stilled as she listened to the desert around her, the sounds so familiar. The low rumble of a semitruck slowing on the I-10 headed east. The yelps and howls of coyotes hunting throughout the many acres of the country club. The cough of someone behind her . . . Endy's eyes widened, and she tensed, ready to jump up and flee.

"Hey, hey. It's just me. Sorry if I scared you," came a soft, low voice from the shadows. And then he came out of the dark, appearing next to her.

Sebastian.

"Mind if I join you?" he asked, his voice like velvet. He stepped closer, then looked down at Endy.

A cloud crossed in front of the moon so Endy knew Sebastian couldn't see her blushing in the momentary darkness. "Not at all," she replied. Smiling, she propped herself up on one elbow.

Sebastian gracefully lowered himself onto the grass. She could sense him smiling back at her.

"Sip?" she asked, offering the can to Sebastian. He took it from her, and a jolt of electricity flowed down her arm as his hand brushed against hers.

"I'm not being a creep and stalking or following you," he said after taking a drink. "I was out taking a walk because my knee was starting to feel tight. And I noticed you here."

"Not creepy at all to have a strange man approach me in an empty lot in the dark of night." Endy chuckled.

"True," Sebastian replied with a snort.

"So how's your knee doing?"

"It's better, should be back to a hundred percent in a couple more days." The cloud covering the moon moved on so Endy could see how Sebastian looked at her, a slight smile on his full lips.

"Maybe in the meantime, you and I could go do something again that doesn't require a knee that's only at ninety percent," he said. "Like would you want to go to dinner?"

Endy's heart seemed to stop. Was Sebastian Hall asking her out?

"You want to . . ." she started to say. But then she could only just stare at his light eyes, more gray than blue in the darkness of night, and that tousled dark brown hair resting against his chiseled cheekbones.

"I mean, we don't have to do dinner," he said, looking away. "We could just go for another ride around the club in the golf cart or something. I don't want to—"

"Sebastian . . ." Endy softened, her eyes bright. "Yes, I do want to. Whatever it is, the answer is yes."

He gave a low chuckle, a warm sound that made Endy shiver. Reaching out, he grasped her hand, his thumb caressing her palm. A beam of moonlight played across them, and Sebastian tucked a loose strand from her high ponytail behind her ear. He gazed at her, a crooked grin playing at his full lips.

"Enchanting Endy." Their eyes locked and Endy felt like she was floating on a cloud. Sebastian collected her other hand, and he pulled them both up to their feet. He towered above her and wrapped his arms around her as Endy reached her arms around his neck. They fit together perfectly.

Mmmmm, thought Endy. *This feels so good, so right.* She tilted her face up to Sebastian's, their eyes still locked. He lowered his face to hers, his luscious lips parted.

Endy closed her eyes and leaned into Sebastian, her heart pounding . . . just as a cold blast of water hit them. The *sssssssh-chk-chk-chk* of the water sprinklers rang out as they started on their automatic timers.

"Gah!" shrieked Endy, as she pulled away from Sebastian.

Water shot left to right, catching them across their heads, backs, and thighs while Endy held on to Sebastian's arm, helping him limp off the lawn.

Laughing hysterically, they made it out of the range of the sprinklers. Her shirt was wet and clinging, water dripped down her legs, and Endy slipped on the drenched turf, falling into Sebastian.

He steadied her, then twirled her toward him, wrapping her in his arms again.

And then he deeply kissed her like she'd never been kissed before.

18

Sebastian walked behind Endy as she entered the dining room. A spray-painted outline of a gorilla wearing headphones encompassed the entire wall in front of them, and palm fronds decorated the ceiling.

When Endy agreed to have dinner with him, Sebastian was ecstatic. This woman was gorgeous, funny, and completely unpretentious.

And completely different from his ex-girlfriend, Sloane.

The last restaurant that he and Sloane had gone to was the well-known sushi place that opened up in Indian Wells Tennis Garden, overlooking Stadium Court Two. The food was delicious, of course, and the staff had treated them well since Sloane was somewhat of a regular there. They'd even had her favorite chilled bottle of sake waiting at their table when they'd arrived. That dinner had cost Sebastian over $300.

When he'd asked Endy where she wanted to go out for dinner, she'd chosen the place with the gorilla graffiti on the walls. The hamburgers were considered the best in the Coachella

Valley, with the most expensive thing on the menu being the triple patty, triple cheese, triple bacon, loaded burger—and that was barely over twenty dollars.

Waiters rushed around them, carrying trays laden with juicy burgers and fresh green salads. One stopped at the table next to them with a frosty stainless steel carafe from which he poured a thick milkshake into a tall glass. The door to the restaurant opened, and a family of seven crowded at the entrance. The busboys cleared a table and then pushed two together.

Sebastian looked over his menu, then closed it almost immediately. "Do you know what you're going to get?" he asked Endy.

"I do," she replied and immediately closed her menu too. "I really recommend the fries here. They're legendary . . . and they're bottomless."

Sebastian raised his eyebrows. "Bottomless?"

Endy nodded and rubbed her hands together. "All you can eat, baby."

Sebastian chuckled and looked over Endy's slender but muscular arms. "You don't look like you take advantage of bottomless fries."

"They're my downfall," Endy said. "In fact, you've got to do me a favor and stop me from going overboard. When I look like I've had enough, please stop me. Not one more fry goes into my pie hole when I get the look."

Sebastian laughed. "You have a *look* when you've eaten too many fries? How will I know?"

"Oh, believe me . . . you'll know."

The waiter placed their burgers in front of them, followed by a large red plastic basket of french fries that he set in the middle of the table. Endy immediately snatched one up and popped it in her mouth.

"Holy smokes," she exclaimed, waving her hand in front of her open mouth. "Hot!"

Sebastian selected a fry, blew on it, then took a bite. "You're right. These are good."

Endy nodded through her steaming mouthful, then grabbed another from the basket.

Sebastian sipped his beer and leaned back in his chair. "So how long have you been the pickleball expert?"

Endy smiled. "Oh, I'm not an expert. And I do other things at the pro shop, too, not just pickleball."

"So you're not an expert?"

"Not by any means," replied Endy. "I'm just an average player. There are plenty of club members who are way, way better than me. A couple have even considered playing on the pro tour."

"There's a pickleball pro tour?" Sebastian asked, his eyebrows raised.

"Yeah," she replied. "Tennis can't have all the fun. I mean, maybe tennis has all the money, but they can't have all the fun, too."

"Is that why you like pickleball so much? The fun?"

"For sure. Well, that, plus the fact that it's so quirky, so approachable." Endy nodded as she spoke. "And so addictive. Someone once told me that they plan their vacations around playing pickleball."

She selected another fry from the basket, popped it into her mouth, and chewed slowly.

"Gary Lombardi told me that after the first couple of lessons and clinics he did, he started playing both in the morning and again in the evening. And then he started carrying his paddle around the house, practicing his groundstrokes." Endy giggled. "Drove Dean nuts."

"Huh," said Sebastian, rubbing his chin.

They continued to talk, mostly about things they enjoyed doing and movies and TV shows they'd watched recently. Sebastian was happy to hear they had shared tastes in movies, and Endy gave her opinion in between eating almost the whole basket of fries.

When the waiter came by and asked if they wanted more, Endy nodded enthusiastically and gave him two thumbs-up. When the basket arrived at their table, she barely waited a minute to let them cool before she started digging in again.

Watching her, Sebastian could barely contain his amusement, but he just sipped at his beer.

"Oh god, I'm so full," Endy said, reaching into the basket again. Her eyes looked a little glazed over and she puffed out her cheeks. Sebastian smiled when he recognized it.

It was the *look*.

Endy took a sip of wine from her glass, then reached into the basket for another fry.

Sebastian pulled the basket away from her. "Uh, you sure you really want another one?"

"Yeah, just one more," Endy slowly said, her eyes glazing

over. She selected a fry from the basket, her hand paused above the table.

Sebastian leaned halfway over the table and grabbed the fry with his mouth, chewed, and swallowed. Then he leaned farther over the table, lifting out of his chair, and bent over Endy, smoothly kissing her.

"Have you had enough?" he asked.

Endy stared into his eyes and warmly smiled at him. "Of what?"

"What do you think?" answered Sebastian, with a lopsided grin.

"I think that they should be bottomless," Endy replied, her eyes twinkling.

19

As usual, when Endy arrived at work the next morning, the first thing she did was look at the schedule. She noticed that she'd been booked for a lesson, but when she saw the members requesting the class, she grew puzzled. All three of the senior-aged ladies were very experienced players.

Endy set out at a jog and headed for the pickleball courts, her ponytail swishing behind her. When she arrived, she saw The Grands. Earlene, Nora, and Candi gathered at the net, each wearing huge grins.

"Did you all book me for a lesson?" she asked.

Nora giggled and nodded, her pure-white curls bobbing.

Feeling suspicious, Endy's eyes shifted back and forth before joining them at the net. "Okay . . . I mean, what can I even teach you?" She looked from face to face to face. Earlene tilted her head mysteriously, and Candi just shrugged.

"Should we maybe move back to the baseline?" asked Endy, still puzzled.

"Or we can start at the net," replied Candi, biting her lip to keep from smiling. "And you can teach us dinks." She smoothed her spiky gray hair under her visor.

"Candi, you all know how to dink," protested Endy.

Candi's lips twitched. "There's dinking," she said, "and then there's *dinking*."

Endy's forehead puckered, and her eyebrows drew together over her sunglasses. "I'm really not sure what's going on here, but I'm not going to argue with you. Dinks it is," she replied.

She held her paddle waist high. "As you all know, the dink is a finesse shot. We try to hit up and get it to land just over the net in your opponent's non-volley zone."

Endy hit the pickleball gently over the net, crosscourt to Earlene, who dinked it across to Candi, who dinked it crosscourt to Nora, who dinked it across to Endy, who dinked it back crosscourt to Earlene, who dinked it across to Candi, who dinked it crosscourt to Nora.

The four players easily hit dinks back and forth between them in the pattern without pausing.

Finally, Candi, still hitting the ball in a gentle arc over the net, said nonchalantly, "Endy, the girls and I have noticed you spending time with a very handsome young man, and we're a bit curious."

Nora giggled and nodded.

Earlene returned the ball to Candi. "All that messy dark brown hair. Yum yum."

"Oh my god," Endy exclaimed as she caught the ball in her hand, stopping the lesson. She put her hands on her hips. "Did you ladies seriously book a lesson with me just so you can find out about my love life?"

"Us? Noooo," replied Candi.

"Maybe," said Earlene at the same time.

Nora just giggled and nodded.

"You know how much you mean to all of us. We're always looking after your best interests," said Candi. "So please don't be mad at some old biddies."

Endy's heart melted, and she smiled warmly at the trio. "I could never be mad at you three," she said as a loud cheer came from the pickleball courts behind them. "So, you have me for another half hour. What do you want to know?"

Earlene grabbed hold of Endy's hand and pulled her toward a picnic table under the awning. She retrieved an insulated cooler from underneath, flipped the top open, and pulled out a pitcher of orange juice and a bottle of champagne.

"Mimosas! We have just enough to last us a half hour," Earlene said, tucking her oversized Dri-FIT T-shirt into her Bermuda shorts.

Nora smiled and nodded.

"You gals are irresistible," Endy said as she reached around and pulled them into a group hug. "I'm incredibly lucky to have you looking after my best interests, but I have a long day ahead of me, so I'll stick with water."

"Fine, be that way," said Earlene. "But start spilling the beans. Tell us everything. How did you meet? How long have you been dating?"

"More importantly . . . how is he in the sack?" asked Nora.

Endy choked and sputtered on the water she was drinking.

"Your young man reminds me of one of the players from Greece who traveled in for the Indian Wells tournament," said

Nora in a high, breathy voice. "What was the name of that one?" She tapped a finger against her lips. "He was a fabulous lover. Could go all night."

Earlene huffed. "Nora, you never needed to know their names."

Nora giggled and nodded.

Endy hid a smile behind her hand. "I'll just share with you that I met him here at the club. I guess he's just visiting. He's a fantastic tennis player—"

"Tennis," said Candi with a grimace. She pulled the visor from her head and ruffled her gray hair.

"We've only gone out a couple of times," continued Endy. "And his name is Sebastian."

"We know," Candi said, and all the ladies smiled.

Earlene put her hands over her heart. "It's still very early in your relationship—"

"I wouldn't exactly call it a relationship at this point," Endy countered.

"Nonetheless, it's very early," continued Earlene. "Keep us posted as things progress."

"We'll book another lesson so we can get updates," Candi chimed in.

Nora raised her mimosa in the air. "Here's to Sebastian," she said as the other two raised their respective glasses.

"I'm crossing my fingers for you," she continued with a slow wink, "that he's Greek."

20

They were late starting the hike. It had been sweltering all week with temperatures climbing up over 110 degrees that day. But Endy had promised to take Sebastian to one of her favorite places in the desert, so they'd waited for the cooler temps later in the day.

Nestled deep within the rocky crevices of the San Jacinto Mountains, Angel Creek Trail was a farther drive and much less traveled than other hiking trails in town such as Tahquitz Canyon or Araby Trail. When they arrived, the sun painted the desert landscape with hues of orange and pink against the rugged terrain, showing off the area's beauty.

"You're sure your knee is healed enough?" asked Endy, as they shouldered their day packs. She took a swig of water from her stainless steel water bottle.

Sebastian nodded. "Completely. Thanks for planning this hike; I haven't been up here before." The crunch of gravel beneath their hiking boots echoed through the stillness of the desert. "So far, it's pretty stunning."

They came upon a family plodding along slowly. The young son ran ten feet forward, came back to his parents, then ran ahead again, kicking rocks along the way of the narrow path winding through the bunches of Joshua trees and gnarled shrubs. The scent of sagebrush hung in the dry air, releasing its fragrant aroma as they passed by.

Sebastian reached out and took Endy's hand, his long fingers entwining hers, then pulled her close and kissed her temple. Tall wild grasses bordered the narrow trail, and the loose sand poofed up with each step they took. The hills in front of them rose up brown and tan, the base lighter with yellow grasses and chunky gray boulders, and the occasional call of a distant bird was sharp in the quiet vastness.

Still following the family, Endy stopped in her tracks, squeezed Sebastian's hand, and pointed midway up the hill at a cluster of rocks on the steep canyon walls.

"Do you see it?" she whispered. Looking to where she pointed, Sebastian smiled widely.

"Wow," he exclaimed under his breath as they watched the bighorn sheep perched on a high boulder, watching them watch it. Nearby, other sheep blended into the hillside, taking small, sure steps toward the bighorn.

Sebastian turned to see if any other hikers followed them, ready to point out the impressive animals, but the trail behind them was empty. When the bighorn sheep moved behind the rock, dropping out of their sight, Endy and Sebastian resumed hiking. The trail meandered in front of them, through the desert expanse, the terrain gradually shifting from coarse gravel to softer sand.

The family in front of them tired early, the toddler already being carried on her father's shoulders, and they soon turned back, smiling at Endy and Sebastian as they passed.

"Looks like the trail is all yours," the father said, holding on to his daughter's legs as they dangled on either side of his neck. "How far are you two going up?"

Sebastian raised his eyebrows at Endy and shrugged.

"Not too far," Endy replied.

The father eyed Endy's backpack. "Good. Looks like you planned for this crazy heat wave we're having and have plenty of water." He wiped the sweat from his forehead. "Be careful and have fun."

"We will." Endy smiled. "We already are."

The sun was making its way west across the sky, the distant outline of rugged mountains emerging on the horizon. The dipping sun cast elongated shadows that danced across the trail, creating a mesmerizing play of light and dark. And without the family in front of them, Endy and Sebastian picked up their pace.

After watching the family hike away, Endy gazed up at Sebastian. "Cute family," she said. "Do you have brothers and sisters?"

Sebastian shook his head. "No, it's just me—only child. How about you?" He opened his water bottle and took a long drink.

"I have an older sister who lives up in Washington. We're pretty close, but I really only see her every couple of years, usually when I need a hand with moving." She smiled. "In fact, she might be coming down here soon to help me pack."

Endy explained to Sebastian that the owners of her casita were planning on selling their property in a couple of months, so she would be moving out soon.

"How do you feel about that?" asked Sebastian, pushing his hair back from his damp forehead. "About having to move out so soon?"

"It's fine. I'm used to it," Endy answered with a shrug. "I'll take a couple of days off from work, and my sister and I will pack up a half-dozen boxes and then spend the rest of the time in the pool with wine, catching up." After a couple of steps, she looked up at Sebastian. "What about you? Do you move around a lot?"

"Yeah, you could say that," Sebastian said with a light chuckle. "I mean, I did move around quite a bit because my father was a foreign service diplomat, and we lived in a bunch of different places before I even got to middle school."

"Seriously? How was that?"

"It was okay, mostly. A little tough being the new kid in the middle of a school year, that's for sure. But in the schools I went to, all the other kids were in the same position I was. We all were often the new kid," replied Sebastian. "But if anything, friendships formed super quickly, because we never knew how long it would be until someone's dad got transferred and they'd have to move again."

They rounded a curve in the trail and came upon an area where the vegetation was less dry, with green leaves stark against the usual browns. The air was cooler and carried a subtle moisture, a change from the start of the trail, and the rhythmic babbling of a distant creek sounded near.

Endy lifted the hem of her tank top and mopped at the sweat across her cheeks. "So you said you moved around a lot before middle school. What'd you do then?"

Sebastian swept his hand through the air, mimicking a tennis stroke. "Have you ever heard of sports academies?" He slid a glance at Endy. "One called IMG Academy?"

"In Florida? Yeah, a bunch of tennis pros trained there when they were young."

"Well, me too."

Endy gasped. "Oh my gosh, Sebastian. How did that—"

"My parents realized when I was around ten or so that I was more than decent at tennis. I'd been taking lessons pretty much my entire life, even when we lived in all those different countries." Sebastian shrugged. "But when I was going into middle school, my dad got this promotion that had him doing three-month stints all over the world for a few years, and my parents knew it was going to be hard on me. So we applied to IMG, and I was accepted to the boarding school and tennis program." Sebastian paused, then said with a half smile, "I was about eleven when I moved there."

"And how long . . ."

"Until I was eighteen and graduated from high school," Sebastian said. "It was the longest I'd ever lived in one place."

"That's a really big deal," replied Endy, her eyes wide with wonder. "*You* must have been a big deal." She stopped and looked up at Sebastian.

"Yes, Endy, I was a big deal. A very, very, very big deal." He grinned and pulled her close, grabbing and tickling her. "Very . . ."

Endy slapped at Sebastian's hands, her laughter ringing off the tight canyon walls. Sebastian leaned closer and kissed her lips, then pulled her tight and kissed down her neck.

"Oh, Sebastian," murmured Endy. She reached up and with one hand, cupped his face, while she stared deep into his sky-blue eyes. Her thumb brushed across his lips, and she said, "I can't wait for you to see it. We're not far."

Sebastian smiled and brushed back a strand of hair from Endy's forehead. "Alright," he agreed. "Let's keep going."

They continued hiking, with the trail tilting steeper and the gurgling of a stream growing louder. The scent of damp earth and the cool mist carried by a slight breeze lifted Endy's hair off her sweaty neck. The trail rounded a huge granite boulder, sticking out from the wall of the canyon.

Endy jogged ahead of Sebastian and stopped in her tracks, an enormous smile on her face. She shrugged her backpack from her shoulders, dropping it to the ground.

"Ta-da! We're here."

Endy spread her arms wide and turned to face a majestic waterfall framed by towering rocks, thundering down from thirty feet above them. The powerful water poured through an opening between two boulders, forming a sheet that splashed violently in the basin beneath it, loud and fierce. Radiant sunbeams flared across the wall of granite, the bright reflection warming a small beach surrounding a crystal-clear pool.

"Wow, Endy," exclaimed Sebastian, his face filled with awe. "This is amazing!" He grabbed hold of Endy's hand and pulled her into his arms, resting his chin on the top of her head, both of them gazing out to the waterfall. He turned her face to his and brushed his lips against hers, then pulled her all the way around and pressed closer to her, kissing her more deeply.

Endy brushed her lips down Sebastian's neck and nibbled behind his ear, getting a response from him that sounded like a cross between a sigh and a moan. She reached up and brushed a long strand of chocolate-brown hair from his forehead, and she ran her fingers down his cheek.

Endy grinned. "Come on! No one's around; let's go in." She twisted away from Sebastian, pulling her tank top over her head. She stepped out of her hiking shoes and shorts and ran into the water. "Gah!" she shrieked. "Cold!"

Sebastian laughed as he lowered to the ground, untying his boots. By the time he'd tossed his shirt on the rock next to the basin and waded into the pool, he'd lost sight of Endy.

"Hey!" he yelled. "You okay? Where are you?" Sebastian moved smoothly toward the waterfall, taking long strides. "Endy?"

The water deepened so Sebastian had to tread while he searched the area beyond the falls. The water bounced up and sprayed his face as he swam. He gnawed at his lip, turning circles, searching for Endy.

And then he saw her.

In a shallow hollow, hidden from view behind the waterfall, Endy stood naked, glistening in a bright beam of golden sunlight.

Her long, dark hair cascaded, dripping over her shoulders, and she pulled it back with her arms upraised, her breasts shimmering wet, her nipples dark pink. She'd tossed her sports bra and panties onto a rock at the edge of the pool and stood waiting for him. Sebastian felt his breath quicken.

She looked at Sebastian from under her eyelashes.

"Someone told me that you were a big deal," she said, running her tongue across her top lip. "Come here and show me how big."

Day had barely broken when Sebastian pulled open Endy's front door and stepped out. The air felt fresh and dry against his bare arms.

He stepped over Endy's hiking shoes on the front steps. They had kissed all the way from his parked car to her front door and started pulling off each other's clothes as they came up the steps. Frantic to get inside, Endy had kicked off her shoes, and they lay there overturned, the laces still knotted. Sebastian picked them up and placed them neatly next to the front door before he sighed contentedly.

He stretched tall, extending his arms overhead. His body was sore, his muscles tired, and he knew he'd be running slower at that morning's tennis match, but he smiled to himself. That's what he got for staying the night with Endy and having sex three times, not including at the waterfall.

But he couldn't keep his hands off her. She was an intoxicating blend of beauty and brains, and he couldn't remember the last time that he'd laughed so much with someone. When she smiled, her whole face lit up, and it made his heart swell to watch her. All that, plus her exceptional skill in bed, had Sebastian completely spellbound.

It had been a long time since he'd felt so intensely about something . . . or someone. The past couple of girls whom he'd dated longer than a few months had all been pretty chill at the beginning. But after about the third date, they would each want more from him. Except Sebastian felt like he didn't have anything more to give.

Until this girl, Endy. If it were up to Sebastian, he'd spend every waking—and sleeping—minute with her.

Before even getting dressed, he had sent a text to her saying that he would be on Stadium Court playing mixed doubles with friends who were in town visiting. Maybe Endy could meet up with him after his match or later that day? He smiled, knowing she would wake up to a text from him.

Sebastian had pulled on his shorts and shirt and ran a hand through his disheveled hair. Then he'd leaned over and kissed her forehead as she slept. Her eyelids had fluttered, and she let out this quiet sigh with a little smile. It had taken all his willpower to not crawl back into bed with her.

But he would talk to her later in the morning, and they would set up a time to see each other that day. And, hopefully, the day after that, and the day after that, and the day after that.

21

Maria was still teasing her, giving her sultry bedroom-eye looks, wiggling her eyebrows, and licking her lips. And Endy couldn't help but giggle. When she'd rushed into the pro shop late for work, walking a little gingerly and bow-legged, her friend had immediately guessed what Endy had been doing the night before.

Endy carried a basket of clean towels to the table near the front door. "I'll never be able to look at a waterfall another way," she said, laughing. "What'll happen if we find ourselves at Niagara Falls?"

Maria joined in laughing. "And he wants to see you again. Endy, I'm so happy for you."

"Let's not get ahead of ourselves," replied Endy. "I mean, a guy like Sebastian must have a million girls chasing him. Why would he want me?"

"Maybe you're the one in a million, *amiga*," said Maria. "Anything can happen, right?"

Endy's lips pulled up in a hopeful smile and she shrugged.

"Sure, anything can happen." She picked up an empty box near the front desk and looked around the pro shop. The tables were neatly arranged with stacks of Whisper Hills logo merchandise, white towels, T-shirts, visors, and water bottles covering every inch. Ready to start the day, she pulled out her keys and walked to the shop's entrance just as the telephone gave a shrill ring, breaking the quiet of the morning.

Endy went on and unlocked the building's front door, pushed it open, and looked over the vast grounds surrounding the racquet club. It was another sun-filled day with ultramarine-blue skies, the pro shop was organized and running smoothly, and she'd just had a night of incredible sex with a guy who had already said he wanted to see her again. Endy breathed in deeply, a satisfied smile on her face, then turned and headed, still a little gingerly and bowlegged, for her office.

"You don't have anything to worry about," Maria exclaimed, rushing up to Endy.

"That's the kind of thing you say that makes me worry," replied Endy as she walked back into the pro shop from the hallway.

"¡Ay!" Maria said. "Don't look!" Maria stepped in front of her, blocking Endy's view to the patio overlooking the large Stadium Court. Endy tried to step around Maria, who mimicked Endy's movement, essentially blocking her.

"Maria, what are you—"

The door to the pro shop opened, and a stunning twenty-something woman drifted in, her long, wavy, copper-red-brown hair framing her model-like face and her thin, athletic body looking perfect in a pure-white Fila tennis dress.

She stilled, then removed her sunglasses, orienting herself. Spying Maria, she smiled, her teeth bright and flawless. "Hi, I have a reservation on Stadium Court and I'm just checking in. My name is Sloane."

"Sloane," Maria repeated with a nod, her eyes wide. "Sloane Stewart." The telephone in the pro shop rang, but Maria remained rooted to where she stood.

"Did I hear Sloane's voice?" asked Joel, walking around Endy in the hallway. He grinned and, within four strides, had Sloane in a big embrace. "Man, you look fantastic."

"Fight on," she replied, smoothing her tennis dress over her hips. "How long has it been? Five, six years?"

"Something like that," replied Joel. "Glad to see you're still playing."

"Oh yeah. I'll be playing until I'm ninety." She laughed smoothly. "I'm just branching out at this point."

"Right, can't wait to talk more about that with you and Daniel this afternoon. Do you have a name for it yet? Or are you just going with Junior Tennis Academy?"

"Coming up with the funding was easy compared to coming up with a name." She rolled her eyes, her thick eyelashes fanned out. "We already have financial backing for a full five years but are still working on what to call it."

Sloane walked toward a clothing rack and pulled out a white-and-navy Lacoste tennis sweater. "This is super cute." She turned over the price tag. "And only $220, huh." She looked at Maria, who had not moved. "Can you hold this for me, and I'll come pay for it when I'm done playing? Just put it under my name, Sloane."

Maria swallowed and nodded. "I know."

Joel grinned. "Put it under her other name, *Shorty*."

Sloane lifted an eyebrow. "You're not allowed to call me that," she said. "Only one person has that privilege, and I just about marr—"

The pro shop phone rang shrilly, and Joel walked behind the front desk. "When you guys are done hitting, come back up here and I can drive us in the cart over to Daniel's office," he said before picking up the receiver.

"Sounds good," Sloane replied, shifting her tennis bag on her shoulder. "Is Sebastian already on the court?"

"Uh-huh, he's on Stadium Court," Joel said with a pointed glance at Endy, who was still hidden behind Maria. "He's waiting for you."

Sloane slipped her sunglasses back on. "Best not to keep Sebastian Hall waiting," she replied with a soft laugh.

"Oh please," said Joel. "You used to keep him waiting all the time."

"That was before," breathed Sloane. A sly grin played at her full lips. "*This* time, I'm going to make sure he can have me whenever he wants."

From behind Maria, still hidden from view, Endy watched Sloane and Joel. She raised her hand to her mouth and gnawed at her thumbnail. Who was this stunning friend of Joel's? They seemed very familiar with one another, like old friends, and from how she'd greeted Joel in the typical USC way, Endy could only guess they knew each other from college.

And why did her name sound so familiar?

Suddenly, Endy's heart missed a beat when she realized that this was the Sloane that Joel had mentioned before.

The Sloane that Sebastian had been engaged to.

Endy felt a dull ache in her stomach as she moved to the clothing racks in front of the pro shop windows that overlooked Stadium Court. Her hands were busy moving the hangers, but her eyes followed Sloane.

Sloane had walked—no, glided—onto the court and air-kissed the other two players. But for Sebastian, she had wrapped her arms around his neck and given him a thousand-watt smile as she ran her hands through his hair. The same hair that Endy had been grabbing at five this morning—for the third time. Endy coughed and rolled her neck, hearing a crunching sound from her tight muscles.

Obviously very comfortable with Sloane, Sebastian rested his hand on her waist as they talked with their heads leaned in close, their shared tallness perfectly perfect.

They looked exquisite together. Even when they walked to their positions on court, they stepped in time. And the easy swing of their racquets while they warmed up was poetry in motion. It was evident that Sloane and Sebastian had spent a lot of time together as a doubles pair—and as a couple.

Also, what was Sloane referring to when Joel had asked her about a junior tennis academy and meeting with Daniel? Did Endy hear correctly that they had full funding for five years? How could it be that easy when Endy couldn't even come up with the $25,000 she needed for Picklers?

Maria cautiously approached Endy, and they stood together

watching Sloane warming up her serve. "Cover the front desk for me. I'll go out and slash her tires."

"It's okay, Maria," lied Endy. "She'll probably be gone tomorrow." She took a deep breath and forced herself to move away from the window.

22

Who could have guessed that someone who was an assistant director at a racquet club would be so incredibly busy? thought Sebastian. But he couldn't deny that Endy's days—and evenings—were packed full.

The day after their waterfall adventure, Sebastian really thought he'd have his hours filled with everything Endy. But after he'd vowed to himself to spend as much time with her as possible, it turned out to be easier said than done. Between her full-time job and taking care of Picklers four afternoons a week, it was pretty hard to slide into Endy's calendar. But a few days later, Sebastian had an idea.

"Hey, you guys," he called, waving as he jogged across the grassy area around the pickleball court.

Standing across the net from Paul Rothman, Endy waved, the morning sunshine casting a glow around her. She wore an aqua-blue Adidas tennis dress that hugged her slender body and just skimmed the bottom of her hips. Her dark hair hung like silk down her back, just the way Sebastian liked it.

She pushed her sunglasses on top of her head and a smile lit up her face, causing Sebastian to grin like a fool.

"Don't tell me that you've forsaken tennis to join us for the pickleball clinic," exclaimed Paul with a twinkle in his eye.

"Yeah, no," chuckled Sebastian. "I'm headed to—"

"Stadium Court for mixed doubles with Sloane," interrupted Paul, crossing his arms across his chest. "We know."

The Grands, standing under the shade awning, stared at Sebastian as he approached the court. Earlene peered over her boxy prescription sunglasses, and Candi stood with her weight shifted on one hip, her foot tapping rapidly on the court surface. Nora wrestled with tearing open the wrapper on a granola bar.

Sebastian shifted his eyes to the trio of older women. "Hi, ladies, you're all looking exceptionally beautiful today." And then he turned to Endy and said, "And you look really, really pretty this morning."

Upon hearing Sebastian's words, The Grands seemed to soften, and they turned away.

"Did you just come here to charm the womenfolk?" asked Endy, her head tilted. "Or do you actually need something?"

"I *actually* wanted to see if you were available tonight . . ." began Sebastian, smiling.

"Darn it," replied Endy. "You know that I have Picklers after work."

"Yeah, I know. But I mean like late, late tonight," he replied, his eyes gleaming.

"Oh my god," interrupted Paul. "The meteor shower!"

"Exactly, it's tonight, and the skies are supposed to be clear," said Sebastian. He looked at Endy. "So I thought we could take a blanket out to the middle of the golf course to watch the shooting stars. Do you think you can stay awake until midnight?"

"I'd love to," answered Endy.

"Of course I can," answered Paul at the same time. Then he immediately colored and clapped a hand across his mouth. "Oh my gosh, Sebastian. Obviously, you meant to invite Endy, not some old third wheel."

Still smiling, Sebastian threw up his hands and shrugged. His eyes caught Endy's.

"The more the merrier," he said. "What do you say, Endy?"

"The more the merrier," she agreed. "I only have one blanket, so Paul, you'll have to bring your own. But just not your lovely Prada cashmere one—that should be left at home on your sofa." She laughed.

"It's a date," said Sebastian. "We'll take my golf cart. I'll pick you both up around 11:30."

They laid out their blankets on the close-clipped grass on the championship golf course, but even before they settled, the dark sky lit up with a bright streak crossing overhead. "Did you see it?" exclaimed Endy, clapping her hands. Sebastian leaned over and kissed her temple.

"Beautiful!" agreed Paul. He tugged his Prada blanket flatter, then lay back, crossing his arms behind his head. "I know you told me to leave this at home, Endy, but life is too short to not use cashmere for the special moments."

Sebastian sat in the middle of Endy's blanket, then pulled her into his lap. She shivered when he wrapped his arms around her, pressing her back into his chest. If Endy didn't know better, she would have sworn she was purring.

She tilted her head back against his shoulder, peering up at the jet-black sky, the darkness pressing around them. Coyotes yipped in the distance, their calls sounding somber in the night.

"How many shooting stars do you think we'll see?" she asked in a hushed tone.

"If we're lucky, it could be a half dozen or more," replied Paul.

"Well, I only need one big one," said Endy, "because all the other wishes that I've made on shooting stars have come true." She laced her fingers through Sebastian's. "I don't want to get greedy."

"Look, there's another one," breathed Paul, lifting an arm to point into the darkness. "Endy, you wait for a big one. I'll take all of the littles like that last one and collect them together to wish on when I need to."

"That's sweet, Paul," murmured Endy. She shifted, turning to kiss Sebastian, then crawled off his lap and onto the blanket to lay down between the two men.

Sebastian lay back and stretched out next to her, all three of them gazing at the huge breathtaking open sky, the clusters of stars twinkling. He reached out and held Endy's hand in his, caressing her palm with his thumb.

Paul cleared his throat and quietly said, "The last time I went stargazing with someone was a very long time ago. I bet we were about your age."

"We?" asked Sebastian.

"Gharrett and I," said Paul. "He was the love of my life."

"Is that who you save your wishes for?" asked Endy tenderly.

"Yes, he was the one. I'll spare you all the details, otherwise we'll be here until the golfers come out for their first rounds," he said. "But we met working at Macy's. We were both buyers . . . I was buying sweaters, he was blouses. And we were on a two-week trip to Hong Kong."

Paul shifted on his blanket, pulling one side up to cover him. "Gharrett was recently separated from his wife and struggling with his sexuality. And well, two weeks in the same hotel in a foreign country with plenty of American whiskey and complete anonymity—"

"—traveling alone with a handsome blond who's endlessly charming and interesting," interrupted Endy.

"Right . . . and all that." Paul chuckled. "Well, we fell madly in love."

A shooting star stretched across the velvety night sky, a fleeting whisper as it danced across the heavens. Endy sighed and snuggled closer to Sebastian.

"But the last night we were in Hong Kong, we decided to do some stargazing from the rooftop bar of the Ritz-Carlton, our hotel. We were drinking champagne and holding hands under the table. It was so romantic, just us together, under the stars. But then a waiter came to our table and asked Gharrett his name and room number. Apparently a phone call had come to the hotel for him and the caller was holding on a guest phone at the end of the bar. When Gharrett heard this, he kind of spooked and yanked his hand from mine and ran to the phone. It was his wife calling, and she was distraught. They had young kids, and she wasn't coping well, and she begged him to come home. I knew before he hung up the phone that it was going to be the last time I'd ever be with him." Paul paused and wiped the back of his hand across his eyes. "It was almost like I could hear him from all the way across the bar when he looked at me and said, 'I'm sorry.' So I drained my glass of champagne and then finished his as he walked out of my life." The coyotes' plaintive howls echoed across the golf course.

"He loved you," murmured Endy, ". . . but he just left you?"

"Yes, he just left me," replied Paul, a sadness creeping into his words. "He had someone else that he loved before me. Someone he'd been with for years. Someone he had history with. How could I compete with that?"

Endy reached out and grasped Paul's hand, holding it tight. She blinked quickly as a dazzling comet lit up the sky, reflecting off the tears welled up in her eyes.

"How could anyone compete with that?" Endy softly asked.

23

Endy walked into the Stout House to find it was packed and uncomfortably warm. The odor of a burned hamburger bun drifted in the air, stirred by the multiple ceiling fans. As she walked past the hostess station, she tucked her phone away after replying to a text from Sebastian. He'd asked her to go to lunch at the last minute, and she'd responded that she had a work meeting so wouldn't be able to join him.

"Hey, Joel," Endy said, placing her phone on the table. He smiled, obviously happy to see her. She pulled out the only other chair and slid onto it. "Who else is coming?"

"Nobody," replied Joel. "Just us." Endy slipped him a curious glance but smiled as a waitress set two pint glasses in front of them before walking away.

"I went ahead and got you an IPA too," said Joel, and he pushed one glass toward Endy.

"Thanks, I guess. I usually prefer wine—"

"This is a new local brew. You'll love it."

Endy took a sip, studying Joel. He looked great, with his hair all casually mussed up and his polo shirt tight across his muscular chest. Endy had not failed to notice the waitress checking him out when she'd delivered their beers.

Joel slid a menu across the table, so Endy picked it up and scanned the lunch specials listed. A song by The Weeknd played loudly over the speakers while a busboy cleared a nearby table, the plates clattering as he scooped them into a plastic tub.

Joel cleared his throat. "Did you send back that extra order of tennis bags?" he asked, leaning back into his chair.

"The Wilson ones?" asked Endy, looking up from the menu. "Yeah, those went back yesterday."

"Good." Joel nodded. "Good. And what did you tell Maria about her time off request?"

"Well, I told her it was okay. I mean, it's not every day that her niece has a quinceañera."

Joel's eyebrow raised. "She has, like, a thousand nieces."

Endy chuckled. "Right. But she's super close to this particular one. She only needs one day off, so I'll cover her Saturday shift. It'll be fine."

"Good." Joel nodded. He sipped his beer and looked around the crowded room. "Seems like we are finally going to get a break in the weather. It's been so warm . . ."

"Joel, what's going on? Why are you being so weird?" Endy asked, her eyes squinting.

Joel took a deep breath and leaned forward, his forearms on the table.

"Listen, Endy, I've been thinking . . ." He looked deep into her eyes. "Maybe we should never have broken up. We were a good couple once and, um, I think we should try again."

Endy's jaw dropped and her eyebrows drew together. "What?" she sputtered. "Joel, what are you even talking about?"

"I'm talking about wanting to get back together with you," he replied with a smile.

"I am totally confused," said Endy. "Does your wanting to get back together with me have anything to do with Sebastian Hall showing up and me spending time with him?"

"Don't be silly." Joel shook his head, then reached out and covered Endy's hand with his.

"Joel, I know that you didn't just imply that I'm silly," she said, her eyes shooting daggers at him.

Joel's mouth twitched and he took a sip of beer. "Some women are pretty sexy when they're silly. Kristen Wiig. Anna Faris. Our Wilson sales rep, Summer."

"Joel!" Endy growled. "Don't be gross about someone we work with. I'm going to pretend that you didn't just say that." She shook her head so vigorously that her hair loosened from the topknot on her head and tumbled down her back. "And why would you even consider us getting back together? We're so over and done with."

"God, you're really upset," he said, trying to laugh it off. He reached over and tucked a strand of hair behind Endy's ear. "Couples get back together all the time, Endy. I mean, look at Sloane and Sebastian. They could get back together pretty easily."

"That's not going to happen."

"Are you sure?"

"Yeah, I'm sure," Endy replied with a toss of her head.

"But are you *really* sure?" Joel smirked with an eyebrow cocked.

"Dammit," Endy said, irate. She was *not* really sure that Sloane and Sebastian would not get back together. They certainly seemed perfect for each other, and he had loved her once before, so what would stop him from loving her again? "I wish there was a steak knife on this table because I would completely stab you in the hand right now."

"*Stab me in the hand?*" Joel repeated, his jaw dropping open. But then a huge smile bloomed across his face, he pushed back and bent over the table, laughing uncontrollably. "You're not going to like it when we start going out again and I only have the use of one hand."

Endy covered her mouth, trying to hold back her own laughter. But unable to contain it, she joined Joel, laughing so hard that her shoulders shook and she had to wipe tears from her eyes.

The waitress gingerly approached the table. "You guys ready to order?"

"Yeah, let's order lunch," Joel answered, still smiling. He pushed the menus to the end of the table. "Endy, what are you going to get?"

Endy grinned and blinked twice, purposefully. "The steak salad."

They burst out laughing again while the waitress gave them a puzzled look before quickly taking Joel's order and walking away.

"You drive me crazy," Endy said when she'd finally caught her breath. "And you and I both know that we are *not* going to start dating again."

"We'll see," replied Joel, rubbing his chin. "We'll see."

"I don't know what's up between you and Sebastian Hall, but I'm not the prize to be won in any contest."

"I know that, Endy," he said. "But even if it were a contest, I'd win. I always win against that clown, Sebastian."

24

Endy and Maria unfurled the banner and laid it flat on the hallway floor. A strong vinyl odor wafted around them.

Whisper Hills Country Club
2023 PADDLE BATTLE
Picklers Youth Pickleball fundraiser
Registration open now!

"Smells like money," said Maria, rubbing her palms together. Endy wrinkled her nose. "I think it kind of reeks."

Maria slid her friend a sideways glance. "My *tio* got a banner made for his Taco Tuesday specials. The smell will go away in an hour or so, but the customers stay all day."

Endy nodded. "This better work just as well for us. I'm really worried because even though we've had plenty of sign-ups, those have only brought in about $5,000."

"Have you asked the Jacobses to sign up?"

"Yeah, both George and Dawn already did. They're going to partner with Gabe and Emily Lee. That should be fun for all of them."

Endy had gone down Whisper Hills' pickleball member list and reached out to each of them individually. Steven Markowitz had signed up immediately and even donated an additional $500. But even with most of the sixty slots being bought and the kids' partnerships set, she was still $20,000 short on meeting next year's budget. Endy knew she had an uphill battle, but she was determined to raise all the money they would need. Picklers was very, very important to her.

Maria hugged Endy and said, "Don't worry, the rest of the money will come in from somewhere. Anything can happen, right?"

Endy nodded and crossed her fingers. "Anything can happen."

Joel approached Endy and Maria with a stack of new hats. He looked down at the banner. "Has the school decided what courts Picklers will use when it's not at Whisper Hills anymore?"

Endy put her hands to her forehead and rubbed her temples. "Crap, I haven't even thought about that, Joel. I have no idea."

Maria took the hats from Joel and moved them to the display rack. "Iron Ridge Country Club has twenty pickleball courts—maybe that's a good place for Picklers. My cousin's cousin works there, and I could ask."

Endy shook her head and replied, "Doubtful. Iron Ridge is so exclusive. Nonmembers aren't allowed to play there even as guests. Can you imagine five dozen kids like Paco showing up after school? They wouldn't even open the gates." She took a deep breath and heavily sighed. "Well, I'll just have to start calling around to try and find a new home for Picklers."

Endy still couldn't get over the fact that Sloane Stewart had breezed into Whisper Hills with a fully formed junior tennis academy planned. She'd already secured the money and the facilities, not to mention Whisper Hills' backing and support. Daniel York was over the moon and had already put an announcement on the website and in the monthly newsletter. The phones had been busy at the pro shop, with callers inquiring about the academy.

Compared to Sloane, what did Endy have? A road to remorse and a big headache if she didn't raise enough money to keep her program going, that's what.

Adding to her headache, Sebastian seemed to be spending a lot of time with Sloane. Quite a lot of time. And it seemed that wherever Endy went, she'd see them together.

Once, after doing her rounds of the racquet club grounds, she pulled up to the golf cart parking spots only to see Sloane and Sebastian leaving the Wellness Spa, the scent of eucalyptus trailing behind them. Sloane was polished and glowing, while Sebastian looked loose and relaxed.

Then a day or so later, with the local weekly tennis league matches being played at Whisper Hills, Sloane and Sebastian had taken seats overlooking the courts, watching the older ladies' competition. Working from inside the pro shop, Endy could see them with their heads close, talking in low tones, Sloane's hand always resting on Sebastian's arm or thigh.

Sebastian had even quit suggesting to Endy that they get

together when she got off work. To be fair, she did have to run Picklers, but that was just four evenings a week.

The telephone rang at the pro shop desk. Endy heard Maria take the call and answer questions about the junior tennis academy, ending the call by saying, "I'll leave a message for Sloane Stewart, letting her know to get in touch with you. She'll be here tomorrow morning."

Of course Sloane would be there in the morning. She was there every day, usually with Sebastian.

Sloane Stewart had quickly entrenched herself at Whisper Hills racquet club . . . and also in Sebastian's life. Again.

Endy gnawed at a torn thumbnail.

"Maria, is it just me," asked Endy, approaching the desk, "or does it seem like Sloane and Sebastian are always together?"

Maria frowned. "Kind of," she replied and pulled up the week's tennis court schedule. She turned the monitor toward Endy. Every day for the next two weeks, Stadium Court was reserved for Sebastian, Sloane, and guests.

Endy put her face in her hands.

"You want their reservations to mysteriously get erased?" asked Maria, her finger poised above the delete button.

Endy sighed. "No, it's going to take more than that to get rid of Sloane. I mean, Sebastian seems to be choosing to spend all this time with her. Like, what if he's thinking about them getting back together?"

"Nooo," Maria hissed. *"Estaria loco."* She frowned and tapped her index finger on her head. "He'd be crazy."

"I don't know . . . it's more crazy that he'd choose me over someone like Sloane," replied Endy. "She's so perfectly perfect."

"You don't know what she's like off the courts and outside of tennis. Maybe she's a slob who wears granny panties under her leggings. Maybe that gorgeous hair is really just extensions."

Endy raised an eyebrow.

"You don't know," Maria said, putting a reassuring hand on Endy's arm. "They probably don't even hang out when they're not playing tennis."

"You're right. I really have only seen them together here, at the racquet club." Endy shrugged and nodded. "They probably don't even talk or see each other when they're not here."

"Exactly," replied Maria, nodding firmly.

25

Trivia Nights at the clubhouse were always well attended by a lively and boisterous mix of club members and employees. Endy was again sitting at a table with Maria, Dr. Steven Markowitz, Paul Rothman, and the Jacobses. They called their group The Pink Dinks and all wore shirts in hues of pink with their team name emblazoned across the front. The group was very competitive. So competitive that The Grands had sworn off Trivia Nights "until Earlene turns 110, or we all die off, whichever happens first."

"Endy, I hope you brought your A game," said Steven, leaning across the table. "We really need to beat the Smartinis this month."

"There's no way they are winning again," Endy replied. "I hope we get a ton of questions about Taylor Swift, because I will slay." While it was important for her to contribute in the pop culture category, Endy was really hoping to use the couple of hours to raise more money for Picklers.

"George spent hours today on the internet," said Dawn

as she pulled out her chair. "He found a website called '101 Trivia Questions and the Answers' and was trying to memorize them all."

"Except at my age, I can't remember what I ate for lunch, let alone 101 trivia answers," replied George. Steven laughed and clapped George on the back, which set him into a coughing fit. Dawn rolled her eyes and handed her husband a glass of water.

Endy laughed too and looked around the room at the fliers she had printed and placed on each table with information on the Paddle Battle. Many of the tables were already crowded with people chatting and sipping drinks, but the table closest to the front was not yet full. Daniel York sat there with a few others who were quietly sipping martinis and bourbon, his arm slung over an empty seat next to him, a glass of white wine already poured.

Joel stood close to the Pink Dink's table, his arms crossed, surveying the crowd, occasionally nodding to club members seated at their tables or waiting at the bar.

"¡*Ay!*" Maria's eyes grew huge, and she grabbed Endy's arm. "Don't look."

"Don't look at what?" Endy turned toward the entry and immediately spotted what Maria was looking at.

Sloane Stewart floated into the dining room wearing a silky cream jumpsuit that complimented her gorgeous coppery hair. A sophisticated older woman, looking polished and stunning in matching cream linen, was on her arm . . . Barbara Tennyson. All eyes in the room were focused on them as they walked toward Daniel's table.

And two steps behind them was Sebastian.

Endy choked and quickly turned to Maria. "What are they doing here together?" She yanked the hot-pink scrunchie from her topknot and shook out her hair, raking her fingers through, trying to tame the tousled mess. She smoothed the front of her T-shirt and gathered the hem, tying a knot at her waist. Endy was mortified at how she looked compared to Sloane's effortless style.

Maria hissed as Joel waved the group over to their table. "Barbara," greeted Joel as he leaned in to kiss Barbara's cheek. He moved aside. "You know Endy, right?"

"Ah yes, hello, Miss Andrews," said Barbara. Endy could feel Barbara's cold gaze, taking in her fuchsia-colored T-shirt and the scrunchie puffed around her wrist.

Joel stepped up to Sloane and air-kissed both cheeks. "Fight on," she greeted Joel.

Maria made a gagging sound and crossed her arms over her chest.

Sebastian walked behind the group, greeting and shaking hands with Paul, Steven, and George. He leaned close to Dawn and kissed her cheek, then did the same to Maria. When he neared Endy, his eyes crinkled and he reached out and tugged at the T-shirt's knot at her waist.

"You're the cutest Pink Dink in the room," he said and kissed Endy's cheek. Her heart skipped and Endy felt their familiar chemistry and attraction as her hand brushed Sebastian's. She longed to throw herself at him and have his strong arms wrap around her.

Joel, with his hand still on Sloane's shoulder, turned to Endy, then cleared his throat and said, "I don't believe you two have actually met. Endy, this is Sloane Stewart. She's going to be running our new junior tennis academy." Sloane turned toward Endy with a wide smile. Her long, thick eyelashes fanned out and her lips shimmered with gloss.

"Sorry I'm crashing your party," she said, her eyes looking past Endy to the other guests in the room.

"Well, it's not really my party," replied Endy gesturing out at the stage. "It's Trivia Night."

"I mean, it's just a perfect time for Barbara to introduce me around." Sloane caught the eye of a sophisticated older couple, and she smiled and waved. "Oh, there's the Daleys . . . and the Russos."

Barbara shifted closer to Sloane. "Sloane's new program is certainly going to appeal to many members who've spent years playing tennis here and are ready to give back."

"Of course, I know so many of them already. But it can't hurt to broaden my outreach and bring in even more funds for the junior tennis academy."

"That's actually what I'm trying to do tonight," replied Endy.

"Endy has put together a great little program for kids in pickleball," Sebastian finally interjected.

"A little pickleball program for kids," said Sloane, wrinkling her nose. "That's *so* sweet."

"*Puta*," muttered Maria, her eyes narrowed.

Barbara smoothed the sleeves of her linen tunic. "That children's pickleball business," she said, "must it be here, at our club?"

"Well, no," replied Endy. "It doesn't need to be at Whisper Hills, but the club has been super generous in providing the courts for free."

"For free?" exclaimed Barbara, her immaculate eyebrows raised.

"Yeah, thank goodness. Otherwise, we wouldn't be able to afford the program. In fact, I'm still trying to raise the final $20,000 for next year. I only have a couple more weeks."

Sebastian smiled. "Well, you should be a little closer to hitting your budget," he said as he slid his hands in his pockets. "Because I just signed up this afternoon."

"You signed up for pickleball?" two voices said in unison. Endy looked at Sloane, who looked at Endy.

"Yeah," replied Sebastian, "with Paco."

"That kid?" Joel snickered. "Good luck with that."

"Why would you sign up for pickleball, for goodness' sakes?" asked Sloane.

"Well, because when I asked Paco who he was partnered with, he told me he wasn't planning on playing. Nobody has signed up with him."

"Have you seen him? There's a reason for that," replied Joel.

"I would have found him a partner," said Endy defensively. Although in truth, she still had not been able to fill all the kids' slots and was in need of more adult players. When she last checked, there were still about ten kids who had not been paired up to play with an adult.

"I know you would have. But I saved you that step," said Sebastian, cocking his eyebrow at Endy. "You can repay me later." Sloane's eyes narrowed, and Barbara pursed her lips. "Plus, you know, pickleball can actually be kinda fun."

It was as if the earth had quit spinning on its axis. Sloane's jaw dropped, and Barbara's eyebrows rose high on her forehead. They stared at Sebastian with matching expressions of absolute horror.

"Oh my god, Sebastian," said Sloane with a mocking laugh. "That's hilarious."

She moved closer to him. "I mean, it's really generous of you to offer your time to that *little pickleball program for kids*." She placed her slender hand on his arm. "So you just go have your teeny tiny bit of fun that day with that child."

"I'm not doing it just for Paco," said Sebastian, a look of annoyance across his face.

"But what other reason could you possibly be doing it for?" replied Sloane. "When the academy gets up and running, you'll offer your time for us and not have to be involved with pickleball."

"Don't tell me—"

"We'll get you settled in when I return from my trip to Bali with my parents," Sloane interrupted, then gazed up at Sebastian. "Remember last time we were there? Come again," she purred. "We can get the same room."

"Sorry, I'm pretty sure I'm busy."

Sloane laughed low. "Really, Sebastian? How busy could you possibly be here? You don't have a job. You don't—"

Sebastian cut her off. "I'm just busy."

"The Indian Wells BNP Paribas Open is gearing up for this year's tournament," said Barbara. "I'm sure I can set you up to be a hitting partner with one of the players. Maybe Taylor Fritz? You know, our families used to be quite close."

Sebastian sighed with exasperation. "Thank you, but I'm fine. I don't need you to set me up. You're not my agent."

Joel placed his hand on Barbara's elbow. "Sorry to interrupt, but it looks like Daniel wants us to go join the table." Barbara turned away from Sebastian, her deep frown quickly erased.

"Sloane," Barbara said, reaching out her hand, "let's go. I'll introduce you to Rob and Melanie Lynch. They just purchased the house next to mine." Barbara grasped Sloane's hand, and they turned toward their table. She called over her shoulder, "Sebastian, come join us. You can meet them as well."

Sebastian took a deep breath and let it out slowly. Before he stepped away, he reached his hand out and cupped Endy's jaw, his thumb rubbing a gentle caress. "I'll call you later," he said, softly. And then he followed behind Barbara and Sloane and smoothly placed a hand in the small of each of their backs.

Pensive, Endy chewed at her thumbnail and slid a sideways look at the handsome trio as they walked away. Sloane was obviously very close and familiar with Barbara Tennyson—enough that they knew the same people, and enough that their outfits matched. And with her invitation for him to join her in Bali, it was also obvious that Sloane was determined to get back together with Sebastian.

The lights in the room flicked on and off, prompting people to move from the bar and head to their tables. The evening's emcee tapped a microphone, testing the volume, then held up his hand waiting for the group to settle.

"Well that was—" said Paul, his fingertips tapping his mouth.

"Uncomfortable," said Steven.

"Bitchy," said Maria.

"—a stunning outfit that Sloane was wearing," said Paul at the same time. The rest of the group stared at him. "I mean, look at how that shade of ivory compliments her coloring." He glanced at Endy and shrugged. "Sorry!"

Endy drew in a deep breath and slowly shook her head. She picked up her full wine glass from the table and chugged. Because not only was that everything her friends had said—uncomfortable, bitchy, and a stunning outfit—but to Endy, that also felt like an indication of what her life could look like in the days ahead.

26

The next afternoon, Endy pulled the golf cart out of the pro shop parking lot. She needed to do her daily check on all the courts to make sure the water coolers were in working order and to look for any maintenance issues. But what she really needed was some quiet time to wrap her head around the fact that Trivia Night hadn't brought in nearly as much money for Picklers as she'd hoped. She was starting to doubt herself, the confidence that she'd had earlier fading. Why had she told Joel that she'd be able to raise $25,000? It probably wasn't going to happen, and not only would she look like a failure and a fool, but it would be the end of Picklers.

Rolling past Stadium Court, Endy spied Sebastian with a smaller figure holding a tennis racquet. A chubby smaller figure.

Endy drove the cart closer and got out just as the boy turned so she could see his face. Baffled, Endy called out to Sebastian as he jogged across the court toward her. "Hey, are you teaching tennis to Paco?"

"Yeah, isn't it great? Remember that time I subbed in and played pickleball with the kids? Well, I noticed how natural Paco was with a paddle and just knew he'd be the same with a racquet. So I had him put my number in his phone and told him that I'd teach him for free."

"But . . . tennis?" replied Endy. "Not pickleball?"

"Yeah, the new junior academy said they'd offer Paco a scholarship for next year."

"Wait, what? Kids in the tennis academy have to pay?" sputtered Endy.

"Of course. It's not pickleball where anyone can just do it. They're so different. Tennis takes tons more time and skill," Sebastian replied. He reached his hand out to Endy. "Hey, did you get my text?"

Endy put her hand to her forehead. "Sorry! I got it, but then Joel asked me about his next lesson, and then one of the club members needed a bag of ice, and then . . . and then I forgot to reply."

"It's okay," Sebastian said, rubbing his chin. "So what do you think? Do you want to hang out after you get off work?"

"I can't." Endy's lips pulled into a pout. "I have Picklers."

"How about afterward? We could go grab—"

"As much as I'd love to, I just have so much to do today," Endy said. "Can we take a rain check? Maybe this weekend?"

"Yeah, maybe," replied Sebastian, reaching out for Endy's hand again. "My friends who are visiting were thinking about going up to Joshua Tree for the weekend. Can I let you know if I'm in town?"

"For sure," agreed Endy with a small smile. She wondered if Sloane was included in the group of friends that Sebastian would be with at Joshua Tree.

"Hey, loser," shouted Paco from the baseline. "Are you gonna waste my time making googly eyes at Endy, or are we gonna play?"

Sebastian chuckled, finally grasping Endy's hand. His thumb caressed her palm. "Stop back in an hour when I'm done so I can make googly eyes at you without an audience." He leaned over and lightly kissed Endy. When he noticed her shiver, Sebastian pulled her closer, flashed her a sexy smile, and covered her mouth with his in a hot, hungry kiss. "An hour, okay?"

"Alright, loser." She smiled, fanning at her face with an open palm. "Do you think maybe when I come back in an hour, I can get more of those?"

Sebastian chuckled, reached out his hand, and tugged twice on her ponytail. "Always more of those for you—anytime, anywhere."

Endy drove the golf cart to the far end of the racquet club property. She stopped on top of a low mound and gazed over the lush green lawn of the championship golf course, watching the palm trees swaying in the desert breeze. Her lips still tingled from Sebastian's kiss, and she thought back to the first time they'd kissed, over on the grass tennis courts. In the days since, they'd become closer, and it seemed to Endy that she was in a kind of dream world. She wondered how she could've possibly caught the eye of someone like Sebastian. Paul Rothman had assured her it was because of her compassion and warmth, but Endy knew those qualities couldn't necessarily compete against things like beauty and success.

From the very top of a palm, a frond detached. Caught by the warm draft, it traveled on the wind, dipping and twisting away, before dropping and getting tangled in the bougainvillea bush below.

Endy took a deep breath and thought about Sebastian going to Joshua Tree with his friends . . . and likely with Sloane. What if Sebastian were the same as that frond, just breezing into, then just as easily out of, Endy's life?

She had fallen hard for Sebastian, more than she wanted to admit. She couldn't help herself. He was so handsome, funny, and incredibly kind. Endy smiled to herself. He was so unlike anyone she'd ever been with, especially Bennett.

But just like with Bennett, an ex-girlfriend had resurfaced. An ex-girlfriend who was beautiful and successful. And very different from Endy.

Sebastian had said that pickleball and tennis were really different. If that were true, it was crystal clear to Endy that she was pickleball, Sebastian was tennis . . . and so was Sloane.

Sloane. Sloane. Sloane. It seemed that every which way she turned, Endy encountered that girl in her flawless flawlessness.

Beautiful Sloane coming out of Daniel York's office as Endy was going in.

Stunning Sloane running on the treadmill, probably on her fiftieth mile, as Endy walked past the gym.

Exquisite Sloane playing tennis every single day on Stadium Court with Sebastian as Endy worked inside, supervising the folding of T-shirts and blending of smoothies.

Sure, Endy knew that Sebastian played tennis every day— sometimes singles, sometimes doubles with Collin or even Joel.

But ever since Sloane arrived, Sebastian had taken to playing mixed doubles, and Sloane was always his partner. Couldn't they switch partners even just once in a while? After all, there was no hard-and-fast rule that said they couldn't.

But Sloane made her own rules when it came to her and Sebastian, even going as far as making sure they wore matching colored tennis outfits whenever they played a more competitive team.

Sloane had breezed into Whisper Hills with her junior tennis academy perfectly planned, just when Endy was struggling with her plan for Picklers Youth League. Then Sloane had roped Sebastian back into spending every day with her. And finally, she had beguiled Barbara Tennyson into being her biggest supporter, this influential club member who had reduced Endy to an afterthought.

Endy not only felt sick to her stomach, she also felt outsmarted.

"Well played, Sloane," whispered Endy to herself, as another palm frond dropped to the ground.

Endy checked the time on her phone. An hour had passed, and she'd done all her inspections. She pointed the golf cart in the direction of Stadium Court, looking forward to spending a couple more minutes with Sebastian. Her tongue peeked out and licked at her lips, and she tried to ignore the butterflies flitting around in her tummy when she thought of being near him.

She heard a peal of laughter as she got closer to the tennis court. Paco stood across the net from Sloane, rhythmically hitting a tennis ball back and forth.

Sloane, *again*. Endy felt her shoulders tense and a frown pulled at her lips.

"Hey, lady, you're a lot prettier than that loser," Paco called out to Sloane, jerking his head at Sebastian. "If you ever get tired of him, hit me up."

Sebastian laughed, then tossed a tennis ball at Paco. It bounced off his feet and rolled off the court in Endy's direction.

"You came back," Sebastian said with a wide smile as he jogged to the golf cart. Before climbing in next to Endy, he picked up a bright green plastic pickleball and a felted green tennis ball from the seat and held both in his massive hand.

Endy studied the balls and then said in a low voice, "You need to choose."

"Sorry?" asked Sebastian as he lowered himself into the passenger seat. "I didn't hear you."

"I said, you need to choose," said Endy. She shifted in her seat. "You need to decide which one you're going to teach Paco."

Sebastian looked taken aback. "Choose? Why do I need to choose? Why can't I do both?"

Endy chewed at her lip. Why? Because she needed Sebastian to get used to the idea of having to pick which he wanted more. Pickleball or tennis. Paddle or racquet. Her or Sloane.

And when it came time for him to make that decision, Endy needed him to choose *her*.

She reached out and took the balls from Sebastian. Her hand much smaller than his, the fuzzy green tennis ball rolled from her fingers, dropped to the floor, and bounced under the golf cart.

"Why? Because there's only room for one," she said softly, closing her fingers around the remaining green plastic pickleball.

27

"Take a walk with me," Joel said, striding into the pro shop from his office. He approached Endy, a serious look on his face, and they walked out of the pro shop and down the path toward the courts. Joel sat down on the wooden bench overlooking the recently constructed pickleball courts.

A heated match played in front of them, with the typical *thwak, thwak, thwak, dink, dinka, thwak* as the players hit and dropped the plastic ball. Three dogs were leashed up under a nearby tree, a bowl of water nearby. The tiny white Chihuahua growled and yapped sharply as they went past.

"What's up?" Endy asked, lowering herself to the bench beside Joel. She couldn't see his eyes behind his mirrored sunglasses, but his lips were pulled in a frown.

"I just got out of a meeting with Daniel," said Joel. He placed his arms on his knees and leaned forward. "He told me that the board received a formal complaint that went to the chairman. It's important enough that they are discussing taking action."

"Action for what?"

"For closing down pickleball," he said, drawing a finger across his throat. "Here at Whisper Hills."

"Joel, that is ridiculous!"

"Is it?" They surveyed the grounds around them. Golf carts parked haphazardly on the neatly clipped lawn, one with its stereo blasting. They'd had to raise their voices over the dogs tied nearby when the Chihuahua began yapping again, setting off the others. Someone had even brought out a portable insulated keg cooler, which sat dripping under the awning.

"We just have to try harder with these guys." Endy waved her hands toward the pickleball players. "You know, get them to tone it down, clean things up."

"We've already tried that, Endy. It's gone nowhere. Our efforts fall on deaf ears."

"But to close it down completely? What will they do with the courts?" But Endy knew the answer to that. They'd revert them to tennis courts. Because tennis was where the money and prestige were. The tennis lessons that Joel taught could bring in over $145 per hour, and he was often booked solid throughout the day. Tennis racquets cost well over $200 each, and a single tennis dress could fetch more than $150. Even Sloane Stewart's junior tennis academy already had full funding.

"Check this out," continued Joel. "Guess who put in the formal complaint."

Endy's eyebrows came together, and she shook her head. "I couldn't begin to guess."

"I'll give you a hint," replied Joel. "We're sitting on their bench." He patted the seat next to them.

Endy leaned forward and then turned around to read the plaque mounted on the back.

In Memory of
CLIVE TENNYSON
Husband. Friend. Tennis Champion.

She gasped. "Barbara Tennyson?" She thought back to the time she'd run into Barbara and been dismissed so completely by her, when she'd dubbed Endy the *pickleball girl*.

Joel slowly blinked and nodded. "She's the sole complainant. The board is meeting in a month to finalize their decision. And I have to be honest with you, Endy," said Joel, his face serious. "I don't actually know what they'll do about your job at the pro shop if pickleball goes away."

Endy closed her eyes and hung her head. How could Barbara Tennyson be so angry that she'd want to shut down a whole pickleball program? And did she really have that much say, that much pull? Probably. There were other Whisper Hills club members who felt the same way she did and would support her, if needed. What had Steven Markowitz called them? *The tennis purists*.

Endy drew a deep breath and bit her lower lip. If the pickleball program at Whisper Hills got shut down and her job got eliminated, Barbara Tennyson would be more than satisfied. She'd get her tennis courts back and be rid of anything having to do with pickleball altogether . . . including Endy.

28

Sebastian limped to his car after coming out of his physical therapy session at the sports club, but his face lit up when he saw her walking across the parking lot. Endy's slender build moved gracefully—he couldn't get enough of seeing her dark, shiny hair hanging across her shoulders and her long legs under her short tennis skirt.

But she looked distracted and seemed to be chewing at her thumbnail, so he moved silently behind her. When he got close enough, he grabbed her from behind and wrapped her in a tight embrace.

"Gah!" she screamed but swatted playfully at his arms when she realized it was him. "There you go again, being a strange man approaching someone in an empty parking lot." She wrapped her arms around Sebastian's neck and lifted her chin to look into his eyes.

Sebastian chuckled. "I'm not so strange."

"I'll be the judge of that," she replied, laughing. "Kiss me so I can decide whether you are or not."

Sebastian pulled Endy closer and pressed his warm lips against hers. He sucked at her lower lip as his hand traveled from her waist down her hip and tugged at her short skirt. "Here I go, being a strange man making moves on a gorgeous someone in an empty parking lot," he whispered against her lips.

Endy leaned into Sebastian's kiss then pulled back with a sigh. "Maybe not so *very* strange, but I'm still a little undecided. Could we take this back up later tonight? I can order a pizza, and we can watch a movie or something," she offered, tilting her head and giving him a seductive wink.

He kissed her temple, then draped his arm across her shoulders, and she reached up, intertwining their fingers. Sebastian frowned and shifted his weight. "Damn, Endy, I wish you would have asked me earlier. I can't tonight since I already have dinner plans."

They headed toward Sebastian's car, but he stopped short and dug his phone from his pocket as it buzzed with an incoming text. When he lifted the screen to read it, Endy saw the name SHORTY across the front.

"Plans?" Endy pulled away from Sebastian and asked, her voice guarded. "Are you going out to dinner with Sloane?"

"Well, yeah," Sebastian said. "There's a group of us, but yeah."

Sebastian saw Endy's face fall, and then she nodded and looked away. "Huh. Well, have a good time."

"Sorry about tonight. It's just that you haven't been available after work," he said, reaching for her hand. "So, I went ahead and—"

Instead of offering her hand, she crossed one arm to the other and rubbed up and down, as if to keep off the cold. "Don't worry about it, Sebastian. I'm fine," she replied with a small frown.

Sebastian squinted at her, pretty sure she was lying to him, especially when she reached her hand to her mouth and started gnawing at her thumbnail.

"Are you sure, Endy?"

"I'm sure. I wouldn't be good company tonight anyway. . . . I have a lot on my mind."

Sebastian studied her while an owl hooted above them, hiding among the jacaranda trees surrounding the dark parking lot. A Toyota truck passed by, and a girl's thin arm waved out the window. "Hiiii, Ennnndddyyyy!"

Endy pulled out her phone and checked the time. "I gotta go," she said, smoothing her skirt over her hips. "Picklers starts in a few minutes."

Sebastian leaned close, lowered his head, and softly touched his lips to hers. "I'm sorry about tonight, but you're needed for Picklers, and that's way more important." He tucked a lock of her hair behind her ear. "You're the pickleball girl."

Endy tensed. Her eyebrows furrowed and she tilted her head as she stared at Sebastian. "What did you say?"

"That I'm sorry about tonight?"

"No, after that." Endy frowned. "You called me pickleball girl."

"And . . . ?"

"Well, there's only one person who calls me that . . . and she's about to ruin my life," said Endy.

"I'm not following. What are you even talking about?" asked Sebastian.

"The only person who calls me pickleball girl is Barbara Tennyson, and she—"

"Bibi?" asked Sebastian. "What's up with you and my grandmother?"

Endy's jaw dropped. "Your grandmother is Barbara Tennyson?"

"Uh, she was last time I checked," replied Sebastian.

Endy's shoulders slumped; she closed her eyes and pinched the bridge of her nose. And then she said, "Fuck."

29

The ambulance siren wailed as it sped past the clubhouse, headed for the back pickleball courts. A fire truck followed closely with lights flashing. Endy and Maria ran to the large window overlooking the grounds, and when they couldn't see what was going on, Endy made for the door.

"This doesn't look good," she said, already on her way out. "Try to find Joel and have him meet—"

"He was on court eight teaching a lesson, so I bet he's already there," replied Maria, her eyes wide. "Get over there! Go!"

Endy turned away and took the stairs two at a time, landing at a run. The players on the tennis courts had gathered at the low fences, craning to get a view of the back, where the emergency vehicles had gathered. With all play stopped, the quiet was eerie, ominous.

A crowd of pickleballers huddled in a circle around the EMTs, so Endy had to push her way through.

On the ground, in the middle of the court, lay Paul Rothman.

"Oh my god," cried Endy. She quickly grabbed Earlene's arm. "What happened?"

"It looks like Paul has had a heart attack." Earlene grasped Endy's hand, bent her head lower, and whispered, "He was playing all out, like he usually does, you know? But after the first game, he was just sweating much more than normal, and he said he felt dizzy and a little nauseous."

Endy put her hand to her chest. "But he didn't stop playing, did he?"

"Of course he didn't," replied Earlene. "He just guzzled down a Gatorade, saying he was probably dehydrated."

Joel threaded through the crowd, finding his way to Endy, his forehead furrowed. "I was over on court eight and saw these guys crowding around Paul. He was already sitting down in the middle of the court—couldn't even make it over to the shade by the fence." Joel drew in a deep breath. "And then he just kind of slumped over. That's when I called 911."

A muscle in his jaw twitched. "I tried CPR until finally the ambulance showed up."

Endy felt her heart breaking. Everyone at Whisper Hills loved Paul Rothman as much as she did. She thought about his teasing ways, always with a sly smile creeping across his lips. She thought about the special times they spent together, all the trivia nights and pickleball games. And then she felt a lump form in her throat when she realized that Paul was all alone, with no one to take care of and watch over him after this ordeal.

"He'll be okay," said Endy, willing it to be true. "He'll be okay."

From across the street, the persistent clanging of a flag's chain beating against its metal pole sounded harsh and grating. A dog's incessant barking carried from a block away.

With tears welling in her eyes, Endy silently pleaded for her friend to do as he had in the past: sit up, say he was fine, and joke that he was just dehydrated. At that moment, with the sun overhead, blazing down on them, Endy found herself shivering.

The EMTs methodically started packing up their portable defibrillator, and the firefighters rolled a gurney onto the court as people stepped aside. The pickleballers seemed to hold their collective breath.

The EMT in charge stood up from his crouch. His eyes searched over the crowd, finally finding Joel and Endy. His lips pressed together, and he gave a short shake of his head.

He mouthed, *I'm sorry.*

After the ambulance took Paul's body away, they all somehow had to continue on with their day. With the news of what happened, the racquet club had fallen unnaturally quiet. The pro shop closed, but Endy still had to show up for Picklers. Her heart was heavy and her thoughts were so much more than sad, and somehow the kids seem to sense it, because they all got along well for once and simply played pickleball. Even Paco was subdued.

When the last kid had been picked up and driven off, Endy puttered about. Wandering onto a grass tennis court, the darkness enveloped her. The lights from the sports courts had clicked off, and the stars were just starting to emerge. She couldn't bring herself to go home to her stark and quiet casita, so she prowled close to the fence, the black windscreens hiding and protecting her.

Endy stumbled across the tightly clipped grass, a heavy sadness weighing on her heart like granite. The court felt empty and desolate, and tears glistened in Endy's eyes as she realized that the empty grass now reminded her that Paul would never again be there to share in moments like the meteor shower. Looking out across the vast expanse of green, Endy found herself drowning, pulled under by the shadows wrapped around her heart.

A train's forlorn whistle sounded far off, fading as it rumbled away, headed east through the desert. Lonely.

Endy's sorrow blanketed her, and finally, she broke.

She leaned her back against the chain-link fence, feeling it scrape her skin as her legs wavered and gave out from under her and she slid slowly down.

Endy covered her face with her hands. She curled into herself, tears flowing down her cheeks. Her shoulders shook with her sobs, the sound drowned out by the many air-conditioning units kicking on, the throbbing hums a loud din in the quiet night.

30

Endy adjusted the stack of empty, folded moving boxes in her arms as she walked through the courtyard to her casita. Clouds lingered from the recent overcast, dark, and gloomy days, obscuring the moon and bringing an unusual desert chill to the evening.

With the news of Paul Rothman's death, the last couple of days at the racquet club had been difficult for everyone. So many of Paul's friends would gather for hours inside the pro shop, talking about how wonderful he was, trading stories of their time together with him.

But hearing his name over and over, Endy's heart broke with each mention. She felt drained; her legs felt as heavy as lead and her body cold.

The cardboard boxes she carried seemed to weigh tons, and she stumbled as she went up the path. Sebastian took three steps out from the dark of the patio and caught Endy in his strong arms. He relieved her of the boxes, placing them on the ground next to their feet, then wrapped Endy tight in an embrace, his cheek resting against her hair.

"What are you doing here?" Endy asked, her voice quiet. "I thought you were playing mixed doubles with Sloane tonight."

"We got an early start and then won the match pretty quickly," Sebastian answered. "And since you and I actually haven't seen each other in a while, I figured I'd see if you were home." Endy's face pressed against his chest, his T-shirt still damp with perspiration from his tennis match. She shivered.

"You okay, Endy?" concern filled Sebastian's voice.

"I'm just so cold." Her voice was so soft he could barely hear her.

"You're cold? It's like fifty-five degrees right now."

"Is it?" murmured Endy.

Sebastian picked Endy up in his arms, cradled her, and carried her into the casita. He laid her down on the lumpy sofa and then walked into the bathroom. Endy heard the water running in the shower, and then Sebastian was standing over her, lifting her up again.

"Let's get you warmed up." He carried her into the bathroom and sat her on the edge of the bathtub. "Lift up your arms," he said.

He pulled her T-shirt over her head, then pulled off her shoes and socks. He worked her leggings down and tossed them aside.

He held out his hand, and Endy grasped it and stood up. Once she was standing, Sebastian reached around and unhooked her bra, then eased her panties down over her slender hips. Endy stepped into the warm cascade of the shower, the hot water spraying on her face. She sighed.

Then the shower curtain pulled back, and Sebastian, naked,

stepped in next to Endy. The steam swirled around them as they stood together, enveloped in the warmth. Endy closed her eyes and leaned her back against Sebastian's chest. He lifted her hair and kissed her neck, and then he turned her around, kissing below her chin, and ran his nose along her jaw to her ear.

"You are so beautiful," Sebastian said softly. His hands rubbed up and down Endy's arms, turning her skin rosy.

She reached her arms up and wrapped them around his neck. She pulled his face down to hers, kissing him hard.

"Are you warm yet?" he murmured, his lips still pressed against hers.

Endy reached out for Sebastian's hand, then guided it between her legs. "Not quite," she whispered, her tongue slipping past his lips.

Endy rolled over, out of the tangle of bed sheets, and patted the nightstand, searching for her phone. She and Sebastian had tumbled into bed, warm from shower sex, and had promptly fallen asleep, their legs twined together, her head on his chest. She felt better, not so cold anymore, but still something bothered her. Something she couldn't put her finger on.

And then the buzzing of a phone had awakened her.

Endy climbed out of bed and pulled a T-shirt over her head, her hair still damp from their shower. In the dark, she searched for the buzzing phone, finally following the sound to the kitchen, where it lay on the counter.

Endy picked up the phone just as the buzzing stopped, and she turned it over. Six missed calls glowed on the phone's screen: two from BIBI and four from SHORTY.

Endy's shoulders sagged and she bent her head, resting it against the kitchen wall. A lump formed in her throat, and the shadows in her apartment seemed to press heavily against her.

She was deathly still when Sebastian stepped into the kitchen. He had pulled on his shorts, and his hair spiked wildly up from sleeping on it while it was still wet. He rubbed his hand across his jaw.

"Hey, you alright?"

Endy looked up, then slid the phone across the countertop to Sebastian. "Your phone was ringing."

Sebastian checked the phone's screen and frowned.

Endy walked away to the living room and stood looking out at the stack of moving boxes still lying in the darkened yard. Sebastian approached her and saw what she was looking at.

"U-Haul boxes?" he asked.

"I told you that my landlords are selling the house, didn't I?" Endy replied.

"But I thought that wasn't for a while, like in a couple of months."

"Yeah, but why should I wait? I might as well start packing now," Endy said.

Sebastian's frown deepened and his eyes grew wary. "But you're just moving to a new apartment," he said. "You're staying in the desert, right?"

Endy leaned forward, her head resting against the window.

She bit at her bottom lip. "I might, but I'm just not sure now. I kind of think it'd be nice to live by the beach or the mountains again. Maybe someplace cooler." She shook her head. "I'm not sure."

"Someplace cooler? You were shivering like crazy earlier," Sebastian said. He paused, staring at the moonlight playing across Endy's face. "Endy, what's really up?"

"I honestly don't know. Maybe I'm just tired . . . tired of caring." She closed her eyes. "I care too much about Picklers . . . and I care too much about my job . . . and I cared so much for Paul Rothman." She swallowed. "And all of it's going to be gone." Endy couldn't bring herself to include that she cared so much for Sebastian, but two other women were determined to keep him away from her, so he would be gone too.

Endy took a deep breath. "I just can't . . ."

"When you say you *just can't*, what does that actually mean? You and me—we're good, right?" Sebastian asked, his jaw tense. "Right?"

Endy looked down at the floor. "Oh, Sebastian, it's obviously not working out with us." She thought of how things were before Sloane had arrived.

"You think it's not working out with us?" Sebastian repeated, staring at Endy, his light eyes intense. "Why would you think that?"

"Well it's pretty clear that Sloane wants back in your life—and, I mean, look at her. You guys are perfect together."

Sebastian raked his fingers through his hair. "Forget about Sloane," he said.

"Forget about Sloane? How is that even possible? She calls you constantly. She texts you constantly. Anywhere I go, you two are together." Endy threw up her hands. "How can I forget about Sloane when you're with her more than you're with me?"

"But Sloane means nothing to me," argued Sebastian.

The phone on the kitchen counter started buzzing again, the screen lit up with SHORTY across the top. Endy looked from the phone to Sebastian.

"Oh, really . . . does she know that?"

"Endy . . ."

Endy tucked a strand of hair behind her ear. "You should probably leave," she said and walked toward her bedroom, closing the door firmly behind her.

31

Over lunch at the clubhouse's patio café, Endy twirled the long-handled spoon in her iced tea, her salad next to her untouched. Around them, golfers leaned back in their rattan dining chairs, ankles crossed, drinking Stella Artois straight from the bottle.

Her phone vibrated and Endy glanced down at an incoming text, the third one from Sebastian since she'd told him to leave her house the night before. She sighed and her shoulders slumped.

"*Que pasa, mi amiga?*" Maria asked, placing her hand gently on Endy's arm.

"Another text from Sebastian," said Endy, shaking her head.

"Well, have you actually talked to him since last night?" asked Maria.

"No, not really," replied Endy. "I did reply to his first text this morning, though."

Maria raised her eyebrows. "And . . . ?"

"And told him that we should call it quits."

"Endy, you broke up with Sebastian through a text?" exclaimed Maria. "That's super harsh."

"It's a thing," reasoned Endy, looking chagrined. "Plus, I honestly don't think I could do it in person." She leaned her elbow on the table and brought her fist under her chin. "Oh, Maria . . . don't you feel like everything is just an absolute mess right now?"

"I mean, sure, you're going through a tiny rough patch."

Endy blew out. "That's an understatement."

"Okay, but we can figure things out. We have each other, bestie. For the past six years, that's what we've done together, and it's been pretty damn good. What's to say these next couple of years won't be even better?"

Endy reluctantly nodded, still looking thoughtful.

"You know what my little cousin Camila says?" asked Maria.

"Tell me."

"She says, 'Don't be sad, Maria, turn that frown upside down.'"

Endy squinted across the table. "You're making that up."

"Well, okay, yes, Camila doesn't say that. She's four years old and an absolute monster. I just made it up." Maria placed her hand on her heart. "But people do say that, and it's how we have to think."

Endy rubbed her chin and tilted her head. "Go on . . ."

Maria sat tall in her chair and declared, "You and me, Endy, are going to turn our frowns upside down." She thumped her hand on the table. "You can stay with me at my cousin's until you find a new place to live. And if they scrap your position here, you can work over at my *tio*'s restaurant until you find something else. And as for Picklers, well, you hand it over to the school with as much money as you can. If you don't have the full $25,000, they'll make do. . . . Sad as it is, public schools are used to budget shortfalls."

"What about Sebastian?" asked Endy.

"Sebastian," repeated Maria. "Well, *chica*, even though you guys didn't work out, I guess just be happy it was good while it lasted."

Endy's lips pulled up in a sad smile.

Maria took a sip of her iced tea. "We'll still find a new group of friends to hang out with, so you won't be lonely when I find some handsome guy who adores me . . . and then we get married, buy a condo, and get a rescue dog."

"That's my dream for you, bestie." Endy lifted her glass of iced tea and tilted it at Maria in a toast.

"Here's to a good man, a two-bedroom condo, and a dog who needs us." Maria clinked her glass against Endy's.

"Anything can happen, right?" Endy said.

"Anything can happen."

At Picklers that afternoon, Endy stood with the kids under the shade awning. Mayhem surrounded her, as was the norm, but everyone was in good spirits, and Endy felt lighter than she had for some time.

Endy sent the kids to their various courts, then turned up

the volume on a Taylor Swift song playing through the portable speaker on the table. She swayed, singing along with the lyrics.

"Endy, I love this song. Can you turn it up?" a little girl shouted from the pickleball court.

"Yup," she replied. Blindly reaching behind her to grab her phone on the bench, Endy stepped on a backpack on the ground, stumbled, and tripped back . . . into strong arms that held her tight in an embrace. She smelled a citrusy, earthy scent, inhaled deeply, and looked up into Sebastian's eyes.

He quickly released her and stepped back, shoving his hands into his pockets. "Sorry."

"Sebastian . . ." said Endy. "What are you—"

"Hey, loser, we're on court five," said Paco from the edge of the patio. He looked from Sebastian to Endy with a troubled look on his face, sensing the coolness between them. "Endy, it's okay if he's here to practice with us, right?"

"Of course, Paco. It's a great idea since you're partnering next week." Her lips pulled into a small smile. "Go ahead. But don't let him cheat."

Paco looked stern. "Boss, we don't cheat. Ever."

"I know that," replied Endy. "I was kidding."

"But we don't, so don't joke about it."

"Okay, I promise." She crossed her heart and looked up to see Sebastian pulling Paco by the side of his collar toward court five, while Paco took swipes with his pickleball paddle at the back of Sebastian's legs.

"Miss Andrews, do you allow spectators?" Endy jerked around to see Barbara Tennyson standing just outside the patio, her hands clasped in front of her. What was it with that family that they were constantly sneaking up on her? "May I go watch my grandson on the far court?"

"Yes, of course, Mrs. Tennyson," Endy stammered. "Feel free to stay as long as you'd like."

Barbara remained still, then slid a glance at the portable speaker. "Perhaps that is just a bit too loud."

Endy rushed to the table and lowered the volume. "I'm sorry. We're just—"

"No, no. It's fine now. Thank you." Barbara nodded her head to Endy, then walked to the bench near court five. She sat down, opened her shoulder bag and pulled out sunglasses and a wide-brimmed hat, then crossed her legs, settling into the seat. Endy thought Barbara looked very at home sitting there on that bench.

Endy spent the next half hour going court to court, reminding the kids that they'd be competing in a week and giving them tips: return the serve deep, try to get to the kitchen, keep the ball low, but if it's popped high, slam it.

When she arrived at Sebastian and Paco's court, she heard Paco call out the score. "Ten, one, two." The first team to reach eleven points won the game, so they only needed one more point. When Paco had called out "two," the third number of the sequence, Endy knew he was the second server on his and Sebastian's team, and they would have to win the next point since teams were only awarded points if they were serving. Endy looked over to Barbara Tennyson, wondering if she was able to follow the scoring system, which might be confusing compared to what she was used to in tennis.

Then Paco delivered a deep slice serve that curved out of the reach of his sixteen-year-old opponent, and their point was easily won.

"Game," he called. Sebastian and Paco tapped their paddles together, then approached the net and tapped paddles with the opponents.

"Nice job, bro," Sebastian said to Paco. "That was fun."

"Come on, bro. That wasn't fun, that was a blowout." Paco scowled. "What's a kid gotta do to get some competition around here?"

"You want some competition?" Endy asked, her lips pulled up in a grin. She pulled out her phone to check the time. "Your mom probably won't get here for another twenty minutes, so let me put together a real match for you guys." She started typing on her phone. "I'm going to let the other kids go, so let's meet back here in a few minutes. Go take a water break."

Sebastian watched Endy head for the shade awning, then nodded once at Paco. "Yeah, go grab some water. I gotta do something, but I'll be back in five minutes." He jogged across the court to where Barbara sat on the bench. Sebastian said something to her, then continued jogging across the street to the large Tennyson property.

Endy made sure the other kids had their belongings and were waiting under the awning for pickup. Once she was sure they were all accounted for, she made her way back to court five where Paco stood with his arms crossed, an angry look on his face. Next to him, stretching his legs, was Steven Markowitz.

Paco approached Endy and hissed, "I told you I wanted to play someone good, and you invited your *abuelo*!" His eyes shot daggers at Endy. "I'm gonna have to go easy on grandpa so he doesn't bust a knee!" Endy hid her smile and shrugged her shoulders.

Out of the corner of her eye, she saw Sebastian crossing the street, carrying a clear acrylic wine goblet. He stopped at the bench where Barbara Tennyson sat and held out the wine to his grandmother. She accepted the glass, and Sebastian leaned over and kissed her cheek.

He jogged onto the court. "Hey, Dr. Markowitz," he said, reaching out and shaking hands. "You joining us?"

"Yes, it appears that Grandpa is, indeed, joining you." He smiled at Paco.

"Who's our fourth?" asked Sebastian, his eyes searching around the court.

Endy held up her hand.

"Really?" said Sebastian, rubbing his chin.

"I mean, if you're okay with it," said Endy, her word carrying a light challenge. "But if you'd rather have someone else join you, I totally understand," she added, worried that Sebastian might be uncomfortable playing with her since they'd just broken up.

"I'm okay with it. What do you think, Paco?" Sebastian asked.

"Bring it," Paco replied, turning his back on Endy and Steven and bending over, wiggling his butt in their direction.

Endy rolled her eyes. "I'll take that as a yes. Are you ready, Dr. Markowitz?" He held up his paddle and nodded. She looked up at Sebastian. "Seriously, Sebastian, are you okay with me playing in?"

The side of Sebastian's lips pulled up in a grin, and he looked deep into Endy's eyes. "More than okay," he said. He walked away, toward the baseline, and called over his shoulder, "Let's go, pickleball girl."

Endy served first, with the ball landing across the court, deep at the baseline. Sebastian hit it back, keeping the ball low, but Steven quickly returned it to the middle of the court. Caught off guard, Paco stuck out his paddle, and the ball popped up above their heads. Endy reached up with her paddle and slammed the ball, hitting the top of Sebastian's feet.

Sebastian burst out laughing. "So that's how it's going to be?"

Endy giggled. She couldn't resist. She turned her back, bent over, and wiggled her butt at Sebastian, which made him howl with laughter. Paco grinned, proud of what he'd contributed to the game. And sure enough, Sebastian seemed more than okay with playing around Endy.

Endy and Steven switched sides, and she served to Paco. He swiped at the ball, which floated over the net. Steven moved forward to return, except the ball landed on the court and skipped away from him, out of his reach.

"Ooohhh," muttered Steven, his arm stuck straight out, far away from the ball. "The boy has a slice."

The air was filled with the squeaking of their shoes as they moved on the court, and the game continued with the four of them shouting and jeering at each other. Each point was hard won, so when a team got a point, the players broke out with arm pumps and yells.

With a tight score at 10–9, the competition was fierce. Sebastian and Paco led, just one point away from a big win.

Sebastian held the ball and announced the score, "Ten, nine, one." He swiped his paddle, sending the serve soaring over the net.

Endy returned the ball then quickly moved forward, coming even with Steven. Her eyes danced and a joyful grin played at her lips. "Nice serv—" she started saying.

But Paco, his forehand in the middle, instantly crossed in front of Sebastian just as the ball bounced in their court.

Thwack! He sent the winning shot hurling through the middle, past both Endy's and Steven's paddles, to win the game at 11–9.

He leaped in the air for a chest bump with Sebastian. Paco stomped his feet and howled, "Aaah-roooooooooooooh!" And he and Sebastian tumbled into each other like young wolf pups.

Endy threw her head back and burst out laughing as Steven dropped his paddle in surrender. "Well done, boys," he called out, raising a clenched fist.

"Aaah-roooooooooooooh!" howled Sebastian.

Endy's heart squeezed in her chest. She had missed Sebastian. And while watching him, thought that perhaps she had made a huge mistake in breaking things off with him. Maybe she was overreacting to Sloane's presence and misconstruing the situation with Barbara's formal complaint.

If Barbara Tennyson was coming around to accepting pickleball due to her grandson Sebastian, then could the program at Whisper Hills be spared? Endy felt a glimmer of hope bubble through her veins. But when Endy looked over to the bench next to the court, her huge smile dropped from her face.

The bench was empty. Barbara Tennyson had taken her leave.

Endy's shoulders sagged. She had thought that maybe by coming by to watch Sebastian play, Barbara would change her mind about pickleball. But she couldn't have been more wrong.

It was obvious that Barbara Tennyson was at the pickleball court supporting Sebastian solely because she cared for him. And Sloane seemed to be at Whisper Hills Country Club for the same reason.

Endy rubbed her forehead and shook her head. In a competition against those two, Endy knew for certain she couldn't win.

32

Hidden by a dense screen of red bird of paradise shrubs surrounding her patio, Barbara continued watching the pickleball game being played on the court across from her home. When she had been sitting on the bench watching Sebastian play with the others, she'd felt so comfortable, so at home. She had spent many hours sitting on that same bench, except her memories were of Clive playing tennis on what everyone considered his own personal court.

When he had retired and left the tour, they had stayed in England to raise their children. Clive managed the money he had earned as a professional, and their investments allowed him to continue being involved in tennis, albeit from the sidelines. But his love of the game made it so that he still played every day, which kept him connected to his partners, and Barbara to their wives and families.

It was his hitting partner's idea to attend the newly formed tournament in California at Indian Wells, so the four of them had booked a long stay in the desert. Barbara hadn't been back to the United States since her parents had passed away, and she looked forward to spending time in the Golden State again.

Stepping off the plane at the Palm Springs airport, Barbara's first impressions were of the blindingly bright sun and the air that immediately warmed her, fading the ever-present chill Barbara had felt for the past twenty years. She breathed deeply, savoring the dry, dusty smell perfumed with hints of sage and orange blossom.

"Clive," she'd said, holding his arm. "I love it here."

Clive surprised Barbara one day, driving her to the middle of a huge empty expanse of desert, just a couple of miles from Sunnylands, the Annenberg estate. They were met in this emptiness by a representative of the new country club that was to be built on the site, Whisper Hills.

Clive had held out a small, teal-colored box, wrapped with a white satin ribbon. "Darling, this is for you."

Thrilled at the surprise, Barbara stood up on her toes and kissed Clive's cheek. She pulled the ribbon loose and removed the lid from the box. Nestled inside was a Tiffany key ring.

"Clive? What . . ."

Clive leaned down and kissed Barbara's forehead. "Welcome home, darling."

The country club representative stepped forward and held out a bundle of large prints, rolled up. "Mrs. Tennyson, I'd like to congratulate you and your husband on being the first residents of Whisper Hills Country Club. You're standing on the site of your future home."

Clive smiled at his wife. "I'd heard that you love it here."

Throughout their entire marriage, Clive had made sure to keep Barbara happy. She was the most important support for him while he played on the tennis tour, city after city, country after country. Barbara was always in his box, watching and encouraging him. Through those hectic years, their relationship stayed rock solid, they always depended on each other, and they remained very much in love.

When their grandson Sebastian was born, it was apparent that he would be a spitting image of Clive, and they were very close and involved grandparents. With Sebastian's parents out of the country for months or years at a time, Barbara and Clive stepped in to fill that role in their grandson's life. They spent all the holidays together, and they would often take Sebastian out of his classes and training at IMG so they could all attend the tennis grand slam events together. Sebastian had grown up on the grass courts of Wimbledon, the clay courts of Roland Garros, and the hard courts at the Australian Open.

But if truth be known, Barbara felt that all their travel and, of course, their age differences were a detriment to Sebastian. He had few long-lasting friendships, and tennis seemed to be his sole and only focus.

Until he injured his knee his junior year at UCLA.

After all the time it took to get him walking without pain, Sebastian had simply given up tennis. And from what Barbara could tell, he'd also given up any sense of purpose or thoughts of the future.

To Barbara, Sebastian seemed incredibly lost and untethered. She worried about him, so when he'd accepted her invitation to come visit for a while, she had a plan to lure him back onto Clive's court and get him interested in competitive tennis again. She had to do *something*.

But then they had taken away Clive's tennis court. And replaced it with pickleball.

33

Sebastian took a sip of coffee. "Everything okay, Bibi?" he asked as he approached his grandmother.

The French doors stood open to the shaded patio. She had always been an early riser, so by the time Sebastian awoke, she'd already eaten breakfast and read the daily issue of the *New York Times*. But her eyes looked bothered, and a slight frown pulled at her lips.

Barbara Tennyson's frown turned into a tender smile when she saw her grandson. "Good morning, Sebastian. Yes, everything is fine. Or rather, I should say that it *was* fine, until . . ."

"Until what?"

"Until those people started up again this morning." She lifted her chin and indicated the pickleball courts across the street. "The mornings are always so peaceful before they arrive."

Happy chatter and the thwacking of paddles on balls carried loudly to where Barbara and Sebastian sat.

Sebastian studied his grandmother. "The noise didn't used to bother you before."

"That's because when your grandfather was still with us, the pickleball courts were farther away, not on—"

"... Granddad Clive's court," answered Sebastian.

"It's not just that they replaced Clive's tennis court for pickleball," replied Barbara. "But that sport is just so disruptive. With the music they play at all hours of the day and night, the drinking and singing, the trash they leave behind." She pursed her lips. "It's boorish."

Sebastian smiled. "Sounds to me like you just described the US Open on the evening before the Finals match."

Barbara huffed and looked away. An ambulance siren's wail carried over the garden wall, moving away, east in the direction of Indio.

"Tennis used to mean so much to you, Sebastian," said Barbara, gently. "Whatever happened?"

"Ah, so this is why you invited me to come stay with you," replied Sebastian, rubbing his chin. "The lame excuse of needing help around the house was just a ruse."

Barbara picked a piece of lint from her sleeve.

"I'm surprised it took you this long to ask, Bibi."

Barbara looked at her grandson with love. "I don't want to pry, you know that. I simply care very much for you."

"I know. And you're right, you deserve an explanation, even if I'm not sure I have one." Sebastian took another sip of coffee. He looked down at his knees, one still wrapped with an ACE bandage.

"It was during that time I had to take off because of my knee injury..." He looked away, his head tilted up toward the majestic San Jacinto Mountains far off in the distance.

She let the pause continue. Sebastian was so like his

grandfather in the way that they both tended to keep their thoughts close to the vest until they had somehow worked through whatever was bothering them. There were times when she would ask Clive a question, and he would merely reply with a nod of his head, acknowledging that he'd heard her. But his reply might not come for days or even weeks. She would not push Sebastian to comment until he was ready.

Barbara looked at her grandson and settled into her chair. She could feel a confession coming, which she knew would not be easy for him.

Sebastian raked his fingers through his hair and thought back to what happened so many years ago. All the work that he'd put into being the best college tennis player on the West Coast, if not in the nation, went down the tubes when he'd lunged for that serve out wide. He'd anticipated it, but Kovacic was on fire that day, and the serve was just too good.

"I spent days and weeks thinking about how I lost that match to Kovacic," he finally said.

Barbara leaned forward and pushed her cup away.

"At first, I felt robbed. And then I was pissed off," Sebastian said, his voice low. "Especially since the rest of the team went on to win. And then the following Monday, everybody was going about their regular lives."

He swirled the cold coffee in his cup.

"But me? I was stuck in my apartment in Westwood. There was no way I could go up and down four flights of stairs with my knee so jacked up."

Sebastian thought bitterly about how he had sat stewing in his torment, alone in his apartment for days on end. After an initial couple of visits from his tennis coaches and some phone calls and texts from his teammates, it seemed as if Sebastian didn't even exist. His team had actually gone on to win the Pac-12 Tournament Championship title without him. They hadn't needed Sebastian at all.

Even Sloane had been busy with school and her own championship matches. She'd barely checked in on him.

He shook his head. "I felt sorry for myself. Nothing is more pathetic than a self-pitying, angry guy with no future. No one could stand being around me, and I don't blame them, but still, I was more alone than I'd ever been."

Sebastian had spent almost his entire life on his own, by himself. Granted he'd been surrounded by coaches and other tennis players at IMG, but it wasn't like he had family by his side. And when he went to UCLA, he'd been by himself then, too. Nothing had changed other than the city he lived in. As long as Sebastian could remember, his "family" consisted of staff, teachers, and other student-athletes.

He had been a tennis player since he was eleven years old. Sebastian didn't know how to do anything else...be anything else.

Tennis had been his identity.

So during those dark days after he'd mangled his knee, he'd realized that it wasn't his injury that was making him so miserable. It was that he couldn't step onto a tennis court, and that essentially rendered him nonexistent. Aside from being a tennis player, what was he? Just another twenty-year-old, business major, washed-up athlete.

Everybody thought that Sebastian had quit tennis. But the fact was, tennis had quit him. Tennis had left him behind.

"Sebastian, I am so deeply sorry," said Barbara, her voice soft. "Where were we? What were we doing? You were so alone and had no support during that time. I had no idea."

"It wasn't just you, Bibi. It was everyone," replied Sebastian. "Sloane didn't even want to be with me anymore. She broke off our engagement pretty fast."

"Sloane did that? Sebastian, we all thought that you were the one to break things off. Why would you allow all of us to be so misled?"

Sebastian's lips tightened into a thin line, and he shrugged. "Even though I'm still kind of bitter about it, back then I thought it would be better for everyone to give her sympathy and for me to be the fool. I didn't fault her. I wasn't the guy she had bargained on anymore."

Tears shone in Barbara's eyes. "Your mother and father, Granddad Clive and I . . . we all thought we were doing the best thing for you, encouraging you in tennis. We thought that's what you wanted."

"You know, I've been told my entire life how similar Granddad Clive and I were. I think that I mostly played tennis because I wanted his legacy to live on with me. Even still, there was a real possibility that I could have been better than he was . . . who knows," said Sebastian.

Barbara bowed her head, one hand over her heart. She held out her other hand, and Sebastian grasped it with his.

"Because tennis was my life, I never thought about finding or doing anything else. Now I have to." He let out a deep sigh. "I guess it's time I did."

"I've always had faith in you, my darling, and your

grandfather would have wanted you to be happy with whatever you eventually decide for yourself," said Barbara. "I will always support you."

"But will you, though?" asked Sebastian, his eyes sad.

"Oh, Sebastian, I failed you once. I promise to never again. *Never.*"

Sebastian leaned over the table and tenderly kissed Barbara's cheek. He rose from the table, collecting their coffee cups, the moment of confession through. Music carried over from across the street, an Ed Sheeran song playing on a tinny speaker.

"What would you like to do today?" Sebastian asked over his shoulder as he carried the cups inside the house.

Barbara smiled at Sebastian's back. "Well, I do need those ceiling light bulbs replaced . . ."

Sebastian peeked his head out the door. "Wait, so you actually need help around the house? It wasn't a ruse to get me here to visit?"

"Of course it was a ruse," said Barbara, giving a dismissive wave of her hand. "We'll leave the light bulbs for the handyman, and perhaps you and I can go have a nice lunch at the clubhouse."

Sebastian chuckled. "Bibi, I'll never be able to figure you out."

"Better men than you have tried," Barbara said with a smile, "and were not successful."

Sebastian walked back onto the patio and leaned against the half wall. A loud cheer came from the pickleball courts, causing Barbara to look across the street, and her smile faded. The winning pickleball players had jumped into each other's arms, chest bumping and grabbing at each other, dancing in a pack.

Barbara sniffed. "Must they gather like that, all crowded together?" she said, irritated. "Like a common mob."

Sebastian leaned against the wall, smiling. "A mob having a great time."

Barbara shot him a sharp look.

Sebastian chuckled. "I'm not trying to argue with you, Bibi. I'm just saying that if a sport can interest all kinds of different people, then it must have some appeal."

Barbara pursed her lips and folded her arms.

"I mean, I find it super fun," Sebastian said, looking thoughtful. "And I'm kind of considering playing it."

"Sebastian, no, you're not!" exclaimed Barbara. *"Pickleball?"*

"Yes, Bibi." He laughed. "Pickleball."

34

It was the last Picklers' practice before the Paddle Battle. The kids were especially riled up, and Endy could barely keep them under control. Maria reached into boxes and frantically handed each kid a tournament-player bag that contained a T-shirt, reusable water bottle, energy bars, and a printed copy of Saturday's schedule. Most kids tore the bag open, with some already pulling the T-shirt over their heads and finishing off the energy bar in a few bites.

"You guys!" yelled Endy over the noise. "Get out to your assigned court. Now!"

Maria raised an eyebrow and shook her head when nobody moved, the chaos continuing. Endy threw up her hands in frustration. But then she pulled her phone out of her pocket and searched her playlist. She tapped the play button, and the music immediately switched from Olivia Rodrigo to Frank Sinatra singing "Fly Me to the Moon."

She turned up the volume, and the kids stopped almost dead in their tracks. Over the music, Endy heard them grumbling.

"Ugh, Endy! What the heck?" someone yelled.

"Why the old guy music?"

Paco made a farting noise with his lips.

Endy grinned. "Get out to your assigned court!" she yelled again, and the kids dropped their bags and scurried out to the pickleball courts, presumably to get away from the painful music playing.

But from the other nearby pickleball courts, where the Whisper Hills members gathered and played, Endy heard a crooning harmony coming from George Jacobs as he held his wife, Dawn, in his arms and swayed her to the sweet sound of Sinatra. Seeing Endy watching them, George blew a kiss her way right before he twirled Dawn under his arm, then dipped her low.

"I'm the luckiest guy in the world," George shouted. "Hoody hoo!"

Endy sighed. The Jacobses had been married for over forty years, and even now they were still so much in love. *Will I ever have that kind of love?* Endy wondered with longing. She sighed again.

Endy stopped at each court and gave instructions to the kids. She didn't want to put undue pressure on them since the Paddle Battle was really a fundraiser, not an actual tournament. Hopefully, real tournaments would come in time, but for now, this event would just be for fun and fundraising.

When she got to the farthest court, she saw only three players—two teenage boys on one side of the net and Paco rushing around the other side by himself.

"That's all you got?" yelled Paco as he ran up and back, side to side. "You guys play like my baby sister."

Endy stopped outside the gate. "Hey, where's your fourth player?" She looked at her clipboard and saw that Brayden was supposed to be with them.

The kids stopped playing, and Paco tapped his paddle against his leg. "He's over on court one. That guy Joel took him."

Endy gazed past all the pickleball courts in front of them to the one closest to the pro shop. Indeed, there was Joel with Brayden, feeding him shots and coaching him on strokes. Endy knew that Joel was taking the competition for the Paddle Battle seriously, and it annoyed her that he had only just started taking an interest in pickleball when it suited him. He wanted to win, pure and simple.

Endy turned back to Paco. "Too bad Sebastian isn't here to sub in," she said. "Was he busy tonight?" Endy wondered if maybe Sebastian had plans with Sloane, and that's why he wasn't at Picklers.

"Nah, he was going to come tonight but texted me and said he hurt his knee again," replied Paco with a scowl. "Tennis can really mess you up."

Endy gave a rueful smile. "Well, pickleball injuries are probably more common, but . . ." Her eyebrows drew together in worry. "How bad is it? Will he still be able to partner with you at the Paddle Battle?"

"Yeah," replied Paco. "He promised he would. He said it's only a little bit hurt and he is just being careful with it until Saturday."

"Oh okay, thank goodness," said Endy, relieved. She looked at the three kids on the court. "There's still fifteen minutes left for tonight. Do you want me to get one of the members to come over and play with you guys?" She pointed over to the courts where the Whisper Hills members played.

At the same time that the two other players chimed in with "yes," Paco grimaced and said, "Oh, hell nah."

Endy looked over the member courts, scanning the players to see who would be a good fourth, when a shrill cry came from the farthest court. All of the pickleball players halted, and heads craned toward the court.

"Oh no," muttered Endy as she ran to help.

Gary Lombardi leaned heavily on the pickleball net, his shoulder drooping. His face paled and his eyelids fluttered.

"Gary, what happened?" exclaimed Endy as she arrived on the court.

Dr. Markowitz approached them and with one look said, "Could be the rotator cuff. Anybody have a bag of ice?"

"No, no, this hurts worse than what ice can do for it," complained Gary. "I might faint."

Endy put her arm around Gary's waist and held him tight as Steven supported Gary's dangling arm. "And I'm pretty sure I'm going to need something stronger than an Advil." They led Gary to a bench, where he gingerly sat down.

"Someone call Dean to come get Gary and bring him to Eisenhower," instructed Steven.

"What time is it? Dean is at his climate change conference event tonight and won't get out until after eight o'clock." Gary whimpered. "Oh, the pain."

"Don't worry, Gary, I'll bring you," volunteered Endy. "Maria can finish up with Picklers while I go get my car." Endy pulled out her phone and texted Maria, letting her know what had happened. "Can someone help Gary to the parking lot? I'll be there in two minutes."

35

They checked in to the emergency room at Eisenhower Hospital, Gary groaning at each step.

"Have I told you how much it hurts?" asked Gary dramatically, his hand to his chest.

"You may have mentioned it once or twice," said Endy, trying not to smile at his theatrics. "Looks like there are more seats in the back of the waiting room. Let's go sit there while we wait for a doctor to see you." Gary leaned on Endy as they walked back, but as they passed a row of seats, an elegant older woman stood up.

"Mrs. Tennyson?" said Endy, slowing her steps. "What are you doing here?"

"Endy?" Sebastian sat in the chair next to Barbara, his leg outstretched across another chair, his knee covered with a bag of ice.

"Oh no, Sebastian! What happened?" Endy bit her lip and concern filled her face.

Gary lowered himself into a chair across from them. "I'm no doctor, but it looks like he hurt his knee."

"Brilliant deduction. Are you *sure* you're not a doctor?" asked Barbara acerbically. She and Gary stared at each other, both with pursed lips.

Sebastian burst out laughing, breaking the frosty tension, and Endy couldn't help but join in.

"Paco told me that you had a very minor injury, so why are you here at the ER?"

"I did tweak my knee yesterday playing mixed with . . ." Sebastian paused and glanced at Endy, ". . . with a group. But it wasn't too bad, and I'd planned on resting it until Saturday."

"But then today," continued Barbara, "he decided to climb a ladder to change a light bulb in my twenty-foot ceiling."

"You did not fall off a ladder at that height!"

"No," replied Sebastian sheepishly. "I tripped carrying it out of the garage."

"I told him he should have left it to the handyman."

"Well, Bibi, how hard could it be?"

Barbara pursed her lips again and pointedly looked at his elevated leg, the ice dripping around his knee. Sebastian glanced at Gary, who stayed silent but nodded once, agreeing with Barbara.

Endy sat in the empty chair next to Sebastian, resisting the urge to hold his hand and tuck back the lock of hair hanging in his eyes. He was so very handsome, and the electricity they shared was still humming, even as they sat in a hospital emergency room.

"Gary Lombardi," said a nurse, walking into the waiting room. "Gary Lombardi, the doctor will see you now."

Gary started getting up, but stopped and said to Sebastian,

"You were already here when we arrived. Why am I being seen before you?" He turned to the nurse to protest.

Barbara stepped toward Gary. "He's waiting for our orthopedic specialist." She stretched out her hand. "I will accompany you with your consultation."

"Orthopedic specialist? I have a rotator cuff injury! I need to see an orthopedic specialist," fussed Gary.

"No, dear," replied Barbara. "What you need is an Extra Strength Tylenol." She held out her hand again. "The two young ones can wait together for Sebastian's doctor."

The swish of the sliding glass doors opening into the emergency room seemed extra loud as Endy sat next to Sebastian in awkward silence. The crepe soles of nurses' shoes squelched across the terrazzo tile floor and machines' shrill beeping could be heard from behind the closed exam room doors. Sebastian shifted in his seat, adjusting the ice bag on his knee.

"You haven't answered any of my calls or texts," he softly said.

"No," replied Endy, looking away.

Sebastian's cell phone buzzed, and a notification showed on his screen.

> at ur house

> where r u

Endy glanced at the name SHORTY above the messages and then gave a resigned shake of her head. It was never going to stop. Sloane and Sebastian were a package deal, doubles partners forever.

The emergency room doors slid open again, a draft of warm air ruffling Sebastian's hair. He pushed a strand off his forehead. "Endy, can we at least talk about it? Why can't we try again?"

"Why?" Endy stood from her chair and nodded at Sebastian's phone. "The answer's on your phone."

"Sloane? We are *not* together, I promise," replied Sebastian. "We don't even see each other that much."

"Yeah sure, and how's that going?" Endy said and crossed her arms. "Sebastian, I've had my heart crushed once before, and I refuse to get Bennetted ever again."

"What the hell does that mean?"

"It means that *I* get to be the one . . . *I* get chosen. Not some ex-girlfriend who comes traipsing back."

"Please trust me," Sebastian pleaded, "I'm not going back to Sloane. How can I change your mind?"

"As long as Sloane is in your life, you can't."

Sebastian covered his eyes with his hand and groaned, then took a deep shuddering breath.

Endy stiffened and then reached out to Sebastian's knee. "Are you in pain, Sebastian?" Endy asked, concerned. "Should I get a nurse?"

Sebastian just shook his head. "No, it's nothing a nurse can help me with."

When Gary and Barbara returned to the seats where Endy and Sebastian sat, Gary looked remarkably less pained.

"This woman is incredibly knowledgeable about shoulder injuries," he said, fawning over Barbara.

"It's not the first time I've been in an ER with a man who has injured his shoulder," Barbara replied with a small smile.

"You're moving so well," remarked Endy. "Did the doctor do some kind of electric pulse therapy or something? I mean, it seems like you're not even in pain anymore."

Gary nodded and slid a glance to Barbara. "The doctor told me it was just a tiny bit pinched, and I'd be fine in a week."

"And they gave him an Extra Strength Tylenol," said Barbara with a nod. She clasped her hands in front of her. "Ah, and who might this handsome gentleman be?" She looked over Gary's shoulder to see someone rushing through the waiting room headed in their direction.

"Hon, I got here as fast as I could," said Dean, reaching out to Gary and kissing him lightly on the lips. "How are you? Is it bad?"

"I'm actually fine, but thank you for coming so quickly. I was lucky to find these guys here. And when I told Barbara what you were doing tonight, she was very interested and invited us to her house for dinner sometime."

Barbara reached out and shook Dean's hand. "Yes, I would be thrilled to have such a respected researcher at one of my dinners. You'll be a big draw."

Dean raised his eyebrows and smiled, nodding toward Barbara.

"And tell me," Barbara said, her eyes locked on Dean's. "Are you also a pickleball player?"

Surprised by the question, Dean tilted his head. "Actually, no. I play tennis."

"Ah," smiled Barbara. "Even better."

Endy moved away from the row of chairs and dug her keys out of her pocket. She looked from Gary to Dean.

"I guess I'll take off since you're here now," she said.

Dean reached out and enveloped Endy in a hug. "Thank you for getting Gary to the ER, and for always looking after all of us. You're one in a million, Endy."

"Just part of the job," she replied. "See you two back at the club tomorrow."

A door opened and a nurse with a clipboard stepped out. "Sebastian Hall? Your doctor will see you now." As Sebastian struggled to his feet, his eyes locked with Endy's.

I miss you, he mouthed. She blinked quickly, then shook her head.

"Goodbye, Sebastian," she said softly before turning away for the exit.

36

Sebastian smoothly pulled the Range Rover onto Bob Hope Drive. The evening traffic was light, with just an occasional Tesla or Porsche passing them.

"I should be driving," said Barbara. "You're the patient with the injured knee."

Sebastian slid a glance to his right. "It's getting dark, Bibi. You know that I don't like you driving at night."

"I don't like it either." She frowned. "Miserable cataracts."

"I appreciate you coming with me to this appointment and insisting on the orthopedic specialist. But I had a feeling my knee wasn't too badly injured."

"Better safe than sorry," replied Barbara. "And as the doctor said, if you continue to reinjure that knee, it might put an end to your tennis playing."

Sebastian changed lanes and nodded without replying. Barbara turned in her seat to look at Sebastian.

"Did you hear what I said?" she asked, crossing her hands in her lap.

"I did."

She reached her hand out to the dash and adjusted the air vent, allowing Sebastian time to continue with an answer. But with Sebastian's two-word response, Barbara knew not to rush him. He'd continue this conversation in his own time.

They stopped for a red light, and Sebastian placed his hand over Barbara's. A brightly lit billboard loomed overhead.

NEED TO SELL? OR WANT TO BUY?
1-800-BUY-SETH
Seth "Seal the Deal" Aldridge Real Estate

"You know, Bibi, I'm really liking living here in the desert," Sebastian said, looking up at the billboard. "In fact, I've been looking at properties." He drove forward as the traffic light switched to green.

Barbara placed her free hand on her chest, a horrified look on her face. "Please tell me you are not working with a random real estate agent that you found from a roadside billboard."

Sebastian laughed. "No, no. Sloane has a friend from USC who has a successful real estate office in Palm Springs. She introduced us, and he's been taking me around to look."

Relieved, Barbara said, "And has Sloane been accompanying you to tour these properties?"

Sebastian shook his head. "No, this is just for me—I haven't invited her along."

He turned onto the road for Whisper Hills. "There's a lot I like about being here. I'm close to you, the weather is fantastic, it's way more chill than being in a big city. I feel like this could be a longer stop for me, maybe somewhere I can put some roots down finally." The Range Rover drove past the security guard booth, and the ornate metal gates scraped as they slowly pulled open. As they approached Barbara's home, landscape lights beamed up, illuminating the trunks of palm trees lining the road and dotting the immaculate borders of shrubs and flowers. Sebastian turned into the driveway of the Tennyson property.

"Well, I certainly love having you here," said Barbara as she squeezed Sebastian's hand. "But you'll need more than just some old woman to keep you company."

Sebastian reached overhead and pressed the button on the garage door opener.

Barbara continued, "What about that young woman from the racquet club pro shop who was at the ER tonight—Endy Andrews? You two seemed to be spending quite a bit of time together."

"Things with Endy are complicated right now, Bibi," said Sebastian.

"I'm sorry to hear that. How so?"

"Well, having Sloane around isn't doing us any favors, and well, frankly, neither is the complaint that you've submitted to the club's board."

Barbara stiffened in her seat.

Sebastian waited for the garage door to fully open, then inched the Range Rover inside. He switched off the engine.

"It's over," he said, a muscle in his jaw twitched. "She doesn't want to see me anymore."

He pressed the button on the remote again, and the heavy garage door lowered, shut tight.

37

He walked up behind her as she sat on the bench next to the pickleball court. The sun dipped behind the mountains, turning the blue sky a deep azure. Around them, air-conditioning units whirred as the afternoon heat continued baking the country club grounds.

"Hey."

Sloane flinched, startled in her seat. "Sebastian! You know how much I hate when you sneak up on me," she scolded, her full lips pulled in a frown.

"Sorry, Shorty, I forgot."

"How could you have forgotten? Time and time again, all those years we were together, and I never got used to you coming up behind—"

"I said I was sorry," interrupted Sebastian. "Jesus, Sloane, you don't have to jump down my throat."

She crossed her arms over her chest and huffed. The thrum of an airplane flying overhead filled the silence between them.

"The text you sent me earlier was very cryptic," Sloane said, turning her head toward Sebastian. "What did you want to talk to me about?"

Sebastian lowered himself onto the bench next to Sloane. "I guess that I've been thinking a lot about us . . . and what's been going on lately," he replied.

"And . . . ?"

"And like . . . I'm wondering what you're even doing here."

"Well, Sebastian, I had this brilliant idea for the junior tennis academy, and Joel offered to help me put it together. He's been super supportive," said Sloane, giving a half shrug. "Honestly, I didn't even know you were going to be in Palm Springs, but . . ."

"But . . . ?"

"But the day I arrived here at the country club, I saw you playing tennis on Stadium Court, and it reminded me of the first time I ever saw you." She placed her hand flirtatiously in Sebastian's lap. "You're still super hot, Sebastian."

Sebastian's upper lip curled, irritation crossing his face. "C'mon, Sloane. You're better than that." He brushed her hand away.

"What's wrong with what I said?" Sloane studied Sebastian through her thick eyelashes. "I mean, why shouldn't we be together?"

Sebastian slowly blinked. "Well, basically, you left me and broke off our engagement."

Sloane shook her head, her copper mane glinting in the afternoon sun. "I was wrong to have done that."

"Were you, though? You must have had your reasons for not wanting to be with me anymore."

"Sebastian, I had it all planned out. We were young and had our whole lives in front of us," Sloane responded. "You were going to turn professional, and I'd travel with you to all your tournaments and help manage your career. Just like what your grandmother did for your grandfather."

"You liked the *idea* of me . . . of me being a professional tennis player. But look at me now. I'm not even a hint of that idea."

"Because you changed everything when you decided not to turn professional," Sloane said as she folded her arms and sat back.

"I didn't just up and decide to not turn pro," snapped Sebastian. "I was *broken*—physically, mentally, emotionally." He jumped up from the bench. "And you abandoned me."

"Abandoned?" repeated Sloane, looking away. "That's a bit melodramatic."

Sebastian's eyes flashed and he raked his fingers through his hair. "Oh my god, Sloane. You didn't want *me* then. Just like you don't want *me* now."

"That's not true."

"It absolutely is true. And what else is true is that I don't want to be with you either." Sebastian let out a harsh breath. "You need to realize that nothing's going to happen between us again."

"But it can if we—"

"*No, it can't.* And you've got to fucking stop calling and texting me." Sebastian stood over Sloane, his shoulders tense.

Sloane bit her upper lip and cast her eyes down, her long lashes brushing the top of her cheeks. Her shoulders slumped, as if she'd wilted. "I know," she said softly, her posturing dissolved.

She shook her head and covered her lips with her hand. A lone raven flew overhead, its large wings casting a shadow across them. "I'm so sorry for what I did to you, Sebastian. I did abandon you. With utterly no guilt on my part, I moved on. It was terrible." She took a deep breath and let it out slowly. "I'm terrible."

He lowered back onto the bench and, with his hand, gently turned her head so they were staring into each other's eyes. "Hey, hey. You are not terrible," he said in a low voice. "It was years ago."

Sloane nodded and searched Sebastian's face. "Do you ever think," she started, "everything would have been different for us if you had been able to turn pro?"

Sebastian leaned back on the bench, shaking his head. "No. In fact, I'm just now realizing that I'm glad my knee got fucked up. I'm glad I didn't turn professional. And I'm glad you broke up with me," said Sebastian. "Even though it's taken me a really long time, I can finally see what I do and don't want."

"You're glad I broke up with you?" replied Sloane. "That's kind of harsh."

"You know what I mean," Sebastian said. "But for the first time in a long, long while, there are things in my life that are really important to me."

Sloane paused a moment before asking, "Is one of those important things Endy?"

"Yeah, it's Endy," replied Sebastian, a line etched between his brows. "But she broke up with me, and I don't know what I can do about it."

"Do you love her?" Sloane asked quietly.

"You know me," Sebastian replied with a wistful smile. "What do you think?"

"Then do what you do best . . . win. Win her back," Sloane said, grabbing Sebastian's hands and clenching them tight. "*Fight on*, Sebastian."

38

Endy could barely push open the door to her office, the floor in front of it was stacked with cases of Gatorade and boxes of bananas and huge canisters of trail mix.

"Help me," came a plea from behind her desk. "Help..."

Endy stepped over the boxes on her floor, leaned on her desk, and peered over. Maria lay splayed out, Endy's desk fan pointed at her face, blowing her curls away from her neck.

Endy smiled. "Did you carry all this up here yourself?"

Eyes closed, Maria nodded.

"And now you're hot and exhausted, right?"

Maria nodded.

"And you want to go home early because you did all the shopping at Costco, then came back here and unloaded and carried it up all by yourself."

Maria nodded.

"Sorry, but I need you the rest of the day because the fundraiser is tomorrow." Endy slid a box of peanut M&M'S to the edge of her desk and tipped it over, spilling the packets next to

Maria. "Oops, looks like this box got accidentally torn open. Maybe if you have a pack or two, you'll get your energy back."

Maria's eyes popped open, and she sat straight up. She grabbed a yellow bag, tore it open, and slipped three M&M'S into her mouth.

"Okay, I'll stay." She fluttered her eyelashes at Endy. "Hey, you know how it's always so busy at Costco? Well, their parking lot was packed full, and I had to park my car across the side street where that big empty storefront was. You know the one I'm talking about?"

"Yeah, wasn't that a Bed Bath & Beyond or something like that? But it's empty now."

"Maybe not anymore. I saw a bunch of construction trucks parked in front."

"Huh. Someone must have leased it out." Endy looked down and moved the multipack box of M&M'S off the sign-up sheet she'd left on her desk the previous evening. Her eyebrows drew together, and she blinked quickly.

"Maria, did you fill these in?" Endy picked up the paper and turned it toward Maria. "All the adult slots have names in them—it's full."

Maria popped three more M&M'S in her mouth and stood up. "I guess I forgot to tell you because I was so exhausted from the Costco run. But yeah, when I was unloading all this stuff, your phone rang so I answered it. Someone named Inez said she and four others wanted to sign up for the Paddle Battle, so I got her info and told her that they could pay the entry fee tomorrow morning when they register and meet their youth partner."

"But we had ten empty spots . . ."

"Yeah, so after Inez called, the phone rang again right after. And it was somebody else who said they wanted to sign up." Maria shrugged. "There were five of them too."

"You're kidding!" exclaimed Endy, jumping up and down. "We're full! We're full! We're full!"

"I know. Why do you think I'm so exhausted?"

Endy pulled Maria into a hug then spun her away. Delirious with happiness, Endy laughed loudly and raised her arms over her head, bumping her hip against Maria's.

"Who's the one with big dink energy now?" she whooped.

Endy was ecstatic. They had all their tournament day supplies ready. The weather forecast for the next day was beautiful and sunny.

And all sixty of her kids would be partnered up at the Whisper Hills Country Club Paddle Battle.

39

The morning dawned just as predicted with the California desert sun shining brightly. The scent of cut grass hung in the air, and families of ducks paddled in the club ponds. In a great mood, Endy admired the sign propped in front of the folding table they were using for registration.

Whisper Hills Country Club
2023 PADDLE BATTLE
Picklers Youth Pickleball fundraiser
Thank you for joining us!

White tents already bookended the table, where parents of the youth players set up drink stations—one with beer, wine, and hard seltzers, the other with nonalcoholic lemonade, iced tea, and bottled water. A ping-pong table waited steps away, across from groups of Adirondack chairs circled around portable propane fire pits. Navy-blue canvas patio umbrellas provided shade, and a sound system with two huge speakers on stands already blared upbeat pop music.

"Where should I put these?" asked Valentina, holding an armload of T-shirts.

"You can bring them over to the registration table," answered Endy. "While you're there, go ahead and check Paco in because we'll be starting matches soon."

"Oh, we checked him in already. He's so excited for this—it's the first Saturday that he actually got himself out of bed and ready to go. He even got me up a half hour early because he said he wouldn't be late because of me."

"He knows us well," Endy replied with a wry smile.

Valentina put her hand on Endy's arm. "Thank you for this . . . for Picklers. I don't know what we would have done with Paco if he didn't have this group."

Endy pulled Valentina into her arms and hugged her hard. "And for me, too. I don't know what I would have done if I didn't have Picklers."

Valentina's eyebrows drew together. "I really hope you're able to keep the program going."

Endy shrugged and sighed, "Anything can happen, right?"

Valentina nodded. "Anything can happen."

The regular Whisper Hills group of pickleball players milled about, an undulating sea of various shades of gray and white hair atop smiling wrinkled faces. The news traveled fast within the group of old retirees, and they were well aware of the formal complaint submitted to the board of directors. All of them came out in support of Picklers, and also to embrace the possible last days of pickleball at Whisper Hills.

Endy mixed between the groups, pausing to hug and thank them for coming. She stopped beside The Grands, who couldn't resist hugging her longer than necessary. A plump woman with gray hair tucked under a hot-pink bucket hat laughed with Candi and Earlene while Nora flirted with a well-toned, very tan, older man with a full head of white hair combed back in a ponytail.

"Hi there," said Endy, approaching with her hand outstretched. "I haven't met you yet. Are you Inez, the one who called and signed up yesterday?"

"No, no, I'm Sharon," she replied. "Candi's sister from Oregon. I'm just visiting and cheering her on. And to be honest, this whole pickleball sport looks like a ton of fun. I'm thinking about taking one of your clinics." She smiled.

Candi elbowed her sister. "Shush! I told you that our pickleball program here at the club may get shut down. Don't make Endy feel any worse about it!"

Sharon colored and clamped a hand over her mouth. "Sorry."

"It's okay," replied Endy. "We're just going to keep going until we hear that we can't anymore."

"That's the spirit," Sharon said. "Goodness sakes, why would they even consider shutting down pickle—"

"PICKLEBALL IS LIFE!" yelled George Jacobs as he pushed into the tent, navigating a stroller containing three yapping black and brown Chihuahuas. "Hoody hoo!"

The many Whisper Hills members loudly cheered in response, sending the Chihuahuas into a frenzy inside the stroller, causing it to tip over. Dumped from their enclosure, the dogs quickly darted away, weaving in and out of the legs of the crowd and causing a gray-haired man to tip back into the table holding bins of bright green plastic balls, which then scattered throughout the tent and rolled down and out across the lawn.

Choking back a laugh, Endy shook her head. "I have no idea why."

Endy picked up a clipboard and scanned the names. The ten late registrants had yet to arrive and pay their entry fee, which made Endy nervous.

"Maria, do you think everyone is here?"

"Yeah, everyone's here."

Endy scanned the crowd in the tent. "But what about that senior player who signed up late yesterday?"

"I'm not sure what you're talking about," said Maria as she sipped a white-peach-flavored energy drink.

"You know, the lady who is bringing four of her friends," reminded Endy. "Her name is Inez."

"Yeah, I told you they're here. They just have to pay."

Endy pulled out her phone from her pocket to check the time. Matches were set to start in a half hour and if the late registrants weren't ready, some of the Picklers kids would be left waiting on the courts. It would be a horrible way to start the fundraiser. Endy gnawed at her thumbnail.

"Next!" Maria hollered. She crooked her finger at a tall twenty-something woman with two knotted braids on top of her head and huge square mirrored sunglasses obscuring most of her face. Her lips glimmered with gloss, and the scent of coconut sunblock hung in the air.

"Hey, you guys ready?" asked Maria.

"Yeah, we're ready," she said and turned to the four girls behind her. Wearing vivid-colored cropped tank tops and short-short skirts, they smiled wide with their full lips outlined in bright shades that matched their clothing. She called out, "Morgan, come up here!"

A young woman with a long blond braid hanging almost to her waist put her quilted backpack on the ground, dug through the interior, then pulled out a soft leather wallet. She approached the registration table.

"This is for me, Morgan," she said, patting her chest. She withdrew two $100 bills, but as if on second thought, took out another $100 bill and handed all of them to Maria. "Go ahead and keep the rest as a donation for the kids' group."

"Wow, that's super generous. Thanks," said Maria, tucking the bills into the cash box. She looked up at the other three girls standing behind Morgan. "You gals ready too?" Nodding, they approached the table holding their wallets, still laughing and chatting.

The noise in the tent amplified as five handsome and fit young men walked up behind the stunning girls, eliciting high-pitched screams and claps.

Pickleball paddles were laid down next to their colorful tote bags. Sweaters and pullovers with various logos made of penguins, horses, and alligators were tossed onto empty chairs. They all hugged each other, and everyone spoke at the same time, their words and laughter mixed together.

Bewildered, Endy gazed out at the group who were falling over each other like adorable kittens in a litter. Who were these people, and where did they come from?

"Okay . . ." Maria took the clipboard from Endy and crossed off ten names. "So with Sebastian's friends' registrations—"

Endy grabbed the clipboard back from Maria. "What are you talking about . . . Sebastian's friends? *What?*"

"Sebastian's ten friends who signed up for this fundraiser." Maria held her arms out wide, gesturing to the crowd of attractive players in front of them. "This crew."

"Wha—"

"I told you that someone named Inez had a group she was bringing. And there were five others who signed up late too."

"Yeah, but . . ." Endy hesitated.

"But what?" Maria slapped at Endy's arm, then pointed to the gorgeous girl with the knotted braids. "*That's* Inez. And those hot guys, they're all Sebastian's friends, too."

Sebastian himself came walking up, clearly stoked to see this crowd. "Hey, losers!" he called out at the group of five buff and handsome guys crowded next to the five fit and gorgeous girls. Greeting squeals of affection rang out as the group saw Sebastian stride into the tent.

"I can't believe you're all here," exclaimed Sebastian.

"This is so much fun!" Inez rushed up and wrapped Sebastian in a hug. "I've been playing, like, all the time at the pickleball center in Santa Monica."

"You have? Pickleball?" asked Sebastian, his eyebrows raised high.

"Yeah, haven't you heard that pickleball's the shit right now?" interrupted a tall, light-haired guy standing next to Inez. He approached Sebastian with a wide smile.

"Wes!" cheered Sebastian. "You're here! I thought you had a tournament this weekend."

Wes tapped his pickleball paddle against the heel of his hand. "I do, but coincidentally, my tournament is being held at Indian Wells. I'm just here to check things out before I head over to play. Gotta support you, bro."

Sebastian closed his fist and tapped knuckles with Wes, then he pulled back and looked Wes head to toe. He grinned. "I still can't believe you're a pro." He lightly slapped the side of Wes's head. "I guess pickleball will take *anybody*."

"You should talk." Wes laughed. "You're the one who invited us all to a pickleball—*not tennis*—fundraiser."

Sebastian threw his head back and laughed. "Can you believe it's not tennis?"

Wes searched the crowd. "Speaking of tennis . . . doesn't Sloane have some kids' thing at this club too?"

"Yeah." Sebastian pulled Wes away from the pandemonium of their friends. "She came in and set up a pretty big-deal junior tennis academy here."

Wes lowered his sunglasses and looked over the top. "So where is the girlfriend?"

"Come on, Wes," sighed Sebastian. "You know Sloane isn't my girlfriend anymore. I don't know where she is."

"But she told everyone that you guys were getting back together," said Wes.

Sebastian scowled. "We were over a long time ago. We are *not* getting back together."

"Huh." Wes slid a glance to Sebastian. "So, would it be okay by you if I ask Sloane to hang out sometime?"

"Oh my god, yeah, of course. Go right ahead. I keep telling

you guys that Sloane and I are over and done with," Sebastian said, throwing his hands in the air. He ducked his head. "Besides . . . I'm hung up on someone else."

"Reallllly," Wes asked with a wolfish grin. "Who is it? Did she play Division I?"

"No, no, not tennis. She's a pickleball girl," Sebastian said and shook his head.

Wes's eyebrows raised high. "Do I know her?"

Sebastian shoved his hands into his pockets and craned his head around to the registration table where Endy stood with Maria. Wes followed Sebastian's gaze.

"So wait, have you been seeing the girl with the long dark hair over there? The one who's in charge?" asked Wes, pointing his thumb toward the table.

"Yep, that's the one." Sebastian nodded, looking at Endy, who gnawed at a pen as she studied the clipboard in her hand.

"Bro, you should have locked that down a long time ago," Wes exclaimed. "How'd you screw that up?"

Sebastian recounted what had caused the rift between him and Endy, starting with Sloane blowing into Whisper Hills and ending with his grandmother's grievance.

Wes rubbed the back of his neck. "Well, all of that sucks, but you gotta do something to get her back."

"I'm trying. Having all you guys here at the fundraiser has brought in a lot of money, so that helps out a ton."

"Well, if there's something else we can do, just ask. It'd be great if *one* of us actually got into a healthy relationship." Wes laughed. "Anything can happen, right?"

Sebastian grinned at hearing one of Endy's favorite sayings. He nodded and crossed his fingers. "Yep, anything can happen."

The atmosphere inside the tent changed as the crowd started moving out onto the lawn and pathways leading to the pickleball courts. A sense of excitement hung in the air, the players buzzing with energy.

"Hope you do great on the tour this year," Sebastian said, wrapping his arm around Wes's neck and pulling him into a big hug. "Hit me up when you're done playing this weekend. I have some things to talk with you about that I think you'll find interesting."

40

Feedback blared from the large speakers outside the tents. "Welcome, everyone! Just ten minutes before the start of the Paddle Battle, so please make your way to your courts. Play starts in ten minutes!" Daniel York's voice boomed from the microphone.

Endy's eyes widened and she took a deep breath. All the time and energy she'd put into planning and putting the fundraiser together was finally coming to a head. She was proud of what she'd accomplished, regardless of whether they made their financial goal or not. The fact was, she considered the crowd of people around her to be personal friends, and they had shown up to support her. Endy felt very fortunate.

"¡*Ay!*" Maria burst out. "Don't look!"

"Ugh, every time you say that, it means—" Endy stamped her foot then turned around with a grimace. "Hi, Sloane."

"Hi, Endy," said Sloane at the same time as she approached the table. "Sorry to crash your party but—"

"It's not my party," replied Endy, blinking slowly and shaking her head. "It's the Paddle Battle fundraiser."

"Right. Well, that's why I'm here. I wanted to give you some advice." Sloane pushed her sunglasses on top of her head.

"*Puta,*" hissed Maria from behind the table. "Just because you and your tennis program came in here with bags of money doesn't mean that Endy needs any kind of advice from you."

Sloane pursed her lips and raised one eyebrow at Maria. She lowered her sunglasses, then crooked her finger at Endy and stepped away from the registration table. "Endy, let's talk over here, away from *tu molesta hermana pequeña.*"

Maria's mouth dropped open, and her eyes narrowed. "No one except my cousins are allowed to call me *their annoying little sister.*" She huffed and tossed her hair. "And you know what? Your accent sucks."

Endy threw up her hands and followed Sloane. They stood in a sliver of shade from a palm tree.

Sloane pulled out her phone and began tapping. She glanced over her sunglasses at Endy and said, "I'm Venmo-ing my donation for Picklers to you."

Endy's eyebrows drew together. "Sloane, you don't have to do that."

Sloane tucked her phone into the pocket of her skirt. "I know, but I want to," she replied, looking down. She waited a beat, then said softly, "I want you to take it as a type of apology. It's my way of saying how sorry I am."

"Sloane, what are you even talking about?"

"Endy," started Sloane. She bit her lip. "I'm leaving Palm Springs for a little bit. Probably go up to LA and meet with more donors . . . maybe take some time to get my head straight." She took a deep breath.

"I'm still not following," said Endy, shaking her head in puzzlement.

"I'm not good at this, so please, just listen," Sloane said, her voice slightly strained. She reached out and placed her hand on Endy's arm. "I . . . am . . . sorry."

Endy's eyes widened. "Sloane . . ."

Sloane's lower lip trembled, and she whispered, "Make him happy."

"You mean Sebastian?" Endy asked, her eyes questioning.

"Of course I do." Sloane nodded. "And the advice I wanted to give you? Go watch his games," she said. "Pickleball seems to be very important to him."

Endy stood with her mouth hanging open in shock as Sloane turned and walked away.

But then, Sloane doubled back, her fingers wiping the tears from under her sunglasses. "*You* are very important to him," she said as she wrapped Endy in a hug. "He chose *you*. He wants *you*."

41

With the energy of players and fans boiling high, the Paddle Battle was officially underway. Shouts of encouragement, groans at missed shots, along with the upbeat music booming from the speakers, created an exciting, fever-pitched atmosphere.

All of Whisper Hills' pickleball courts were filled with two pairs of senior/junior players, and each played for best two out of three games. Volunteers kept score and tracked each team's wins and losses.

At the end of the fun-filled day, the two top-scoring teams would face off for a championship match to conclude the event. Stadium Court was temporarily re-striped from tennis court lines to mark out a pickleball court, and seating had been arranged around all four sides.

"Endy, I have to hand it to you," said Daniel York as he approached her standing next to a court, watching a game. He held out his hand and shook hers. "This is an incredibly well-attended event. Way bigger than I'd ever thought."

Endy smiled widely. "I know! Never underestimate the power of pickleball."

"That's for sure. Let's go, Picklers." Daniel nodded, pumping his fist. "So, do you know where are you in the money department? How much were you able to raise?"

Endy's face fell. "Unfortunately, not enough. We're still about $10,000 short." Her eyes implored Daniel's. "Please, Daniel, can't you come up with the balance? Even if Picklers isn't run through Whisper Hills anymore, it's such a great program and cause."

"I'm sorry, Endy. You know my hands are tied. We never had Picklers in the budget for more than two years." He looked away. "Not to mention that our own program may get shuttered anyway."

Daniel's phone rang, the sound piercing. He answered quickly then mouthed, *I have to take this*, as he walked away from Endy.

Endy sighed. Her heart was breaking just thinking about telling everyone that these would be the last matches played by the Picklers Youth Pickleball League. But maybe after she handed everything over to the school district, they'd be able to find matching funds or another way to keep any kind of pickleball program going without her and Whisper Hills. It was a long shot, but anything could happen—just like she and Maria always said.

But then there was the dark cloud of Barbara's formal complaint to the board hanging over Whisper Hills' own pickleball program. Endy had told Daniel to never underestimate the power of pickleball, but the actuality was that they shouldn't ever underestimate the power—or fury—of a formidable woman. Barbara Tennyson was so close to getting her husband's tennis court back, as well as all the other pickleball courts resurfaced into tennis courts.

By the time Endy checked in on all the courts, pairs of players were already moving on to their next match on different courts. Matches were going quickly, so with short breaks in between, teams would get four to five matches each. Around midafternoon, by which time most of the pairs were starting their final matches and everything seemed to be running smoothly, Endy made her way to the registration table.

"Hey, how's it going?" she asked. "Everything still okay?"

Maria puffed out air, blowing at the curls drooping over her forehead into her eyes. "It's still busy, but nothing I can't handle." She pulled a multipack box of peanut M&M'S out from under the table.

Endy smiled and grabbed a pouch from the box. "What do the scores look like?"

"All pretty even with most of the teams splitting matches," replied Maria, looking over the score sheet. "Well, except for, of course, Luke Skywalker versus Darth Vadar."

Endy screwed up her eyebrows. "What?"

"Potter versus Voldemort . . . Thor versus Loki . . ."

"Maria, what are you—"

"Taylor versus Kany—"

"MARIA!" yelled Endy. "What in the hell are you talking about?"

Maria stopped and stared at Endy. She blinked slowly and shook her head. "You don't have to yell," she said and handed the score sheet to Endy.

At the top read Joel and Brayden, undefeated with all five of their matches won.

And Sebastian and Paco, undefeated with all five of their matches won.

Tied, going into the championship match.

42

Endy strode toward Stadium Court, where volunteers were making final preparations for the concluding games. The courtside seats were already filled with everyone anxious to watch the championship match. From the sidewalk surrounding the sunken court, Endy looked over the crowd.

George Jacobs caught her eye and blew a kiss her way. Endy smiled and blew a kiss back in return. Nearby, Dr. Markowitz leaned back and chatted with a couple sitting behind him, all of them wearing the Dri-FIT T-shirts they'd gotten for participating in the event. Kids ran, screaming and laughing, across the lawns bordering the court. Endy nodded to herself, knowing she had done a great job pulling these groups together.

At the net, waiting to start the match, stood two tall, very handsome men also wearing the event T-shirts. Next to them were one confident, athletic sixteen-year-old and one dark, chubby pre-teen, gyrating his hips and singing at the top of his voice along to Luis Fonsi's "Despacito" playing from the event speakers.

The noise from the stands quieted as the first game started. Joel and Brayden won the coin toss and opted to serve. The crowd could feel the tension as Sebastian and Joel faced each other, positioned at opposite corners of the court.

"This is my house," said Joel, staring at Sebastian, a smug smile on his face. "You're going down."

Sebastian quirked up an eyebrow, his eyes hidden behind mirrored sunglasses. "Fight on, Joel," he goaded.

A muscle twitched in Joel's jaw. And then immediately after the ref called out, "Game one. Zero, zero, two," Joel dropped the ball, swung his paddle, and served . . . out wide.

Taken off guard with Joel's signature shot, a ball that was wide and far out of his reach, Sebastian lunged toward the sideline, extending his arm and leg. The ball skipped off the floor of the court, and Sebastian tripped awkwardly on his outside leg.

"Fu–!" Sebastian choked back as he landed heavily, off-balance. He grabbed his knee.

"TIME-OUT!" Paco yelled from the middle of their court. He dashed toward Sebastian with concern etched across his face. "Boss! You okay?"

"Time-out?" Joel threw up his hands. "What the hell, kid, we've only played one point!"

Paco turned and stared hard at Joel, flipped up his middle finger, and rubbed it across his chin.

Sebastian took a deep breath, stood tall, and put weight on his leg, testing it. "Yeah, I'm good." He walked to Paco, and they tapped paddles. They gathered at the back of the court, their backs turned to Joel and Brayden. Sebastian bent low, his head close to Paco, listening intently as the kid whispered something.

"Time!" called out the pickleball referee.

Paco stomped to his receiving position on the left side of their court, clutching his paddle tightly with anger.

Joel had swapped sides, and the ref called out the score. "One, zero, two." Joel served the ball over the net and Paco swung his paddle, returning the ball deep. Brayden smacked the ball and moved in as it sailed over the net. Sebastian scooped it up, then softly caressed the ball, dinking it into the kitchen. Joel dinked it back to Sebastian, who dinked it back to Joel.

Dink. Dink.

Finally unable to contain himself, Paco darted in and slapped at a high ball, sending it down the middle past an unprepared Brayden.

The crowd erupted with cheers. Paco turned to the stands and bowed low, then brought his paddle to his forehead and gave a salute. The crowd cheered even louder.

From her vantage point on the sidewalk, Endy locked eyes with Valentina, who was standing next to the court with a hand clapped to her forehead. *This is gonna be looong*, she mouthed. Endy grinned and nodded.

Tension still high, the championship game continued, the two teams evenly matched. The court echoed with the sounds of paddles striking the ball over and over and over. Points were hard-fought, with both teams unwilling to surrender. And as the match progressed, the intensity only grew. Rallies became longer, and the four players executed gutsy moves, returning what seemed like impossible shots.

Sebastian and Paco played with boundless energy. At the end of each point, regardless if they had won it or not, they'd come together and tap paddles. "Let's go," they'd say to each other, pumping their fists.

As Endy watched, she sensed an exuberance in Sebastian that she'd never seen. Since after that first point when Joel had snuck in the wide serve, Sebastian seemed so . . . happy. Radiant, even, like he was bursting with joy. He wore a constant grin that lit up his face, and he laughed with gusto. He played freely, his shots loose and confident.

And after what felt like hours, they were tied at 9–9, with Paco serving next after Sebastian had lost his service game.

"Nine, nine, two," the ref called out.

Paco's serve to Brayden was deep, skidding off the front of the baseline. Brayden jabbed at the ball but didn't connect, and his paddle whiffed through the air.

"Point," declared the ref.

"Come on!" celebrated Paco, and he tapped his paddle to Sebastian's.

Swapping sides, Paco held the ball, waiting for the ref. Joel slid a glance to where Paco's last serve had landed, deep at the baseline. He took two steps back.

"Ten, nine, two," announced the ref. The crowd in the stands quieted.

Paco readied to serve. He dropped the ball again and swiped it with his paddle. Only this time, rather than flying deep, the ball came up short and low. Unprepared for the slice serve, Joel rushed forward but was out of position when the ball hit the ground and twirled to the right. He caught the ball with the tip of his paddle, sending it out of bounds into the stands.

The crowd jumped up from their seats cheering, the applause thundering.

43

"Point. Game," called out the pickleball ref. "Lopez, Hall. Eleven, nine." She jotted it on her clipboard and then walked to the center of the court, where Daniel York stood with a microphone in hand.

"Wow, that's some great pickleball right there!" he whooped, a huge grin across his face. "We're going to take a bit of an extended break to thank our contributors, so hang around and make sure to stay for the rest of this fantastic championship match!"

Music started playing around Stadium Court as Daniel read from a printed list he held in his hand. The four players made their way to their seats while the audience chattered, some heading to the beverage tents.

Endy watched Sebastian lower himself to the bench with a grimace, his hand rubbing his knee. Behind him, wearing her trademark sun hat and cream linen tunic, sat his grandmother, Barbara. She tenderly laid her hand on his shoulder.

Sebastian reached up and covered Barbara's hand with his own. Smiling, she pulled it closer, bringing his hand to her cheek.

Then Barbara leaned in close and said something to Sebastian that caused him to sit up straight. His mouth dropped open in a look of astonishment. Endy saw him take a deep breath, his shoulders softened, and his head bowed briefly.

And then he stood up and pulled Barbara into his arms, enveloping her. But when she tried releasing the embrace, Sebastian extended the hug, trapping her, and wouldn't let go. Barbara tilted her head back and laughed with pure joy and delight.

Endy's jaw dropped. She had never seen Barbara Tennyson look so . . . happy.

Endy's mouth was still open and her eyes wide when she heard her name being called. She backed up, and without looking, turned abruptly, colliding directly with Daniel York.

"Endy, I've been looking for you to tell you—" Daniel started.

"Hey, Daniel," Endy interrupted. "I've been talking to the regular Whisper Hills pickleball members. They're all having such a great time today that they want to have another event in the next week or two. Kind of a send-off for the shutdown of the program and for, you know, the end of my job here."

Daniel grabbed Endy's arm, his eyes excited. "No, no, no. Listen, I have—"

"The Grands said they want to rent out the Victor's dining room, but—"

"No, Endy, that's not going to be necessary because—"

"I know! I told them the same thing. Like, we could just have pizza and beer and that would be more than—"

"ENDY! Stop interrupting me and just listen, because you're not going to believe this," Daniel hollered. He madly shook Endy's arm. "It's been canceled!"

"How can the send-off event be canceled when we haven't even set a date yet?" Endy asked with her eyebrows drawn together.

"Not the send-off event," Daniel said, "the formal complaint."

"The what? Daniel, what are you even—"

"She, Barbara"—Daniel grabbed Endy's shoulders and pointed her body toward where Sebastian and his grandmother sat—"rescinded the formal complaint to the board!"

Endy's eyes blinked quickly, and she stared at Daniel. "Barbara Tennyson pulled the complaint?"

Daniel's face beamed. "Yes! The Whisper Hills pickleball program is back!"

Endy couldn't wait to tell the news to George and Dawn, Steven, The Grands, and all the rest of the regular Whisper Hills pickleball players. She needed to work her way to them in their courtside seats in Stadium Court. But the pathways were crowded with groups of players done for the day and families standing in packs talking.

"Excuse me," Endy said, pushing through the bodies. "Pardon me." Near the beverage tent, she pressed up against a group of attractive young players forming a wall. Obviously friends, they were crowded next to each other, laughing and playfully grabbing and shoving each other.

"Excuse me," Endy said again, pushing forward. She tapped the shoulder of the girl standing in front of her, trying to get past. The curvy girl's dark hair was tied in two knots on the top of her head, and she was arm in arm with a girl with a long blond braid. "Excuse me."

"¡*Ay!* Who's being so pushy?" Maria turned around, her eyes hidden behind huge square sunglasses.

"Maria?" gasped Endy, taking a step back.

"Endy, we've been wondering where you were!" screamed Maria, dropping Morgan's arm and giving Endy a huge hug. She turned to the group. "Everyone, this is Endy!"

"Ennnnddddyyyy!" yelled the blond with the braid, holding up a can of hard seltzer.

"Ennnnddddyyyy," repeated the others. They touched their cans to each other's, then tilted them back and drank deep.

Collin Park leaned out from the beverage tent. "Maria, you want another?" He shook an empty hard seltzer can. "Let's get one more then head back to our seats."

"You have to come sit with us," Maria told Endy, giving Collin a thumbs-up. "Sebastian's friends are so much fun!"

Endy stood still, shaking her head, bewildered.

"Oh, I almost forgot. This is for you." Maria reached into her sports bra and pulled out an envelope with *Endy Andrews, Asst. Director of Racquet Sports* scrawled on the front.

She hugged Endy. "I'll save a seat for you," she called over her shoulder and joined arms with Morgan. Inez came up behind them, draping her long arms over both their shoulders.

Endy's eyebrows screwed together as she studied the envelope. She tore the flap open and pulled out a folded piece of paper. Her jaw dropped.

Inside was a check for $15,000 dollars made out to Picklers Youth Pickleball League, bearing the signature of Barbara Tennyson.

44

The second game was starting up. Fans in the stands stopped dancing and chatting and settled back into their seats. But the atmosphere was still buzzing, and the tension was high.

Endy threaded her way through the row to the empty seat next to Maria, who pulled down her sunglasses and winked. Endy grabbed her hand and squeezed.

The loud music muted, and the referee announced, "Game two. Time in. Zero, zero, two."

With a serious look on his face, Paco nodded to Sebastian, who nodded back. And then Paco served the ball crosscourt to Joel.

Agitated from losing the last game, Joel was more than ready for Paco's serve. He put his weight forward and propelled himself into the court, catching the served ball and returning it just in front of Paco's feet. Paco tried to hit the ball but instead swatted it into the net.

"Come on," Joel said under his breath, with a tight nod of his head.

"Side out! Zero, zero, one," the ref called as Joel and Brayden now got to serve.

Joel caught the ball tossed to him and walked to the back of the court, waiting for Sebastian and Paco to take their places. Then he dropped the ball and served it deep to Sebastian, who returned it and then moved smoothly forward.

Joel caressed the ball over the net, and then Sebastian did the same. Paco and Brayden bounced on their feet, watching, as the ball stayed low and soft. Then Joel flicked the ball wide, and Paco returned it crosscourt. Joel pounced on the ball and hit it so quickly that Sebastian couldn't react. Joel and Brayden got the first point.

Each point was challenging, with the two pairs equal in their play. The score remained tight throughout the game until finally each team was so near to closing out that the tension couldn't possibly get any higher.

"Ten, eight, two," called out the ref.

One point away from winning the game, Brayden took a deep breath. He released the ball and swung hard, but his serve sailed over the net, landing out past the baseline. Brayden groaned, closed his eyes, and his head fell back.

"Side out!" called the ref. "Eight, ten, one."

Sebastian served to Joel, then moved in along with Paco. Joel hit the ball midcourt, and Sebastian smoothly scooped the ball just over the middle of the net. Brayden, with his forehand in the middle, reached for the ball, but Joel rushed forward and darted in front of Brayden and hit a backhand that sent the ball straight into the net.

"Point! Nine, ten, one."

Sebastian and Paco swapped sides. Brayden, seeing that Sebastian was serving to him, took three steps back, far behind the baseline, and was in a great position to take the serve. His return landed midcourt, just as Sebastian ran forward and slammed a forehand right at Joel, whose paddle deflected the shot, sending it out of the court.

"Point! Ten, ten, one!"

"Time-out," yelled Joel. He and Brayden jogged to the back of the court and laid their paddles down. With the score tied, and just two points away from a game win, Joel pulled Brayden close as he whispered some strategy. Sebastian could see the intensity in his face as Joel's hand gestured wildly. Brayden stood still, gnawing at his lip and listening to Joel. Sebastian saw Brayden nod reluctantly, then look up in the stands at his parents. They clapped and pumped their fists, encouraging their son.

The four players jogged to their positions, and the game resumed. Sebastian served crosscourt. Joel connected solidly with the ball, then used his wrist to whip it at an extreme angle, back crosscourt, and . . . out wide.

Taken off guard by the angle and velocity of the ball, Sebastian abruptly leaped right, desperately lunging for the ball. His muscular arm stretched and extended all the way, his hand gripping his paddle. His leg stretched out to cover the momentum, and he landed violently, jamming and twisting his knee.

Sebastian's leg buckled under him, and he dropped to the

ground, his paddle thrown away and both hands gripping his knee. "Aggghhhhhhhhhhhhhh!" he screamed in pain.

"TIME-OUT!" yelled Paco, and he rushed to Sebastian. "Ref! Medical time-out!"

Concern etched the ref's face as she spoke into the walkie-talkie. "Medical personnel requested on court."

Within minutes, a medic rushed onto the court, carrying an equipment bag, and knelt next to Sebastian.

"Fifteen minutes," called out the ref.

Endy and Barbara Tennyson had both jumped from their seats and cried out in unison when Sebastian dropped to the ground.

Barbara steadied herself against the back of the seat in front of her while Endy pushed her way through the row of spectators. Once free, she leaped down the steps, her hair flying behind her.

Coming to a sudden stop at the end of Barbara's row, upon seeing her standing, Endy stammered, "Mrs. Tennyson, I can't begin to thank—"

Barbara held up a manicured hand, her large diamond rings glinting in the sunlight. She glanced to where Sebastian lay writhing on the court, then looked deep into Endy's eyes. "Go to him. He needs you."

Endy's eyes filled with tears, and she whispered, "Thank you . . ." She took a deep breath. ". . . for everything." And then she dashed toward the court.

"Ah, if it's not the hot EMT," she said, recognizing the medic from months ago when Paul Rothman had still been alive and had tried setting her up on a date. Endy placed her hand on his shoulder, and he turned, their eyes meeting.

"You!" His lips pulled into a smile, but just as quickly into a frown. "Hey, listen, I'm so sorry about the loss of your friend."

Endy placed her hand over her heart. "Thank you. I miss him."

"You must," replied the EMT. After a pause, he asked, "So, you been on any blind dates with any firefighters or traffic cops lately?"

"No, not lately and none planned," replied Endy with a grin. "And you? How about *your* plans for your wedding in Tahoe?"

Sebastian had pushed up on one arm. "Hello? A little help here?" he interrupted with a grumble. "Medic needed for someone injured?" He threw his hands up and then pointed at his knee.

Chastened, the EMT quickly opened his kit and turned toward Sebastian's outstretched leg. "Sorry, bro," he apologized.

"I'm sorry too, Sebastian," Endy said quietly. She bit her lip and reached her hand out as if to stroke Sebastian's cheek, but quickly dropped it to her side when she saw his eyebrows furrow. Her shoulders drooped, and tears prickled in her eyes.

"For what, Endy?" Sebastian asked, his eyes closed in pain.

"Well, for one, I'm really sorry that you're injured," she replied. She couldn't stand seeing Sebastian in pain, whether it was from his knee getting tweaked or from her turning him away. "And two, I'm sorry that I'm so, so late in offering you an apology."

Sebastian groaned as the EMT lifted his leg. He opened his

eyes and stared deep into Endy's, the pain causing his forehead to wrinkle. "But you're so good at being late."

"I know." Endy sighed and cast her eyes down. She knelt on the court and pushed his hair from his forehead, tucking a dark lock behind his ear. "Sebastian, I'm so sorry because I should have listened to you when you said that you and Sloane were over."

Sebastian nodded, his lips pursed.

"And I'm sorry because I should have been more sure of our relationship, knowing you'd be there for me, even if your grandmother shut down pickleball across the entire world and I'd never get another job."

Sebastian closed his eyes again, a look of pain across his face.

"Sebastian, are you okay? Is it okay that I'm telling you this?" Endy tripped over her words in her worry. She grasped his large hand in hers. "Are *we* okay?"

Sebastian winced. "Tell the hot EMT to give me some Extra Strength Tylenol." Holding her hand still, he twined his fingers in hers. "And you and me? We're more than okay."

Endy exhaled the breath she had been holding, cupped Sebastian's face with her free hand, then leaned down and smothered her lips against his, kissing him deeply.

"My boyfriend needs some Extra Strength Tylenol," she told the EMT, her heart skipping and her sparkling eyes never leaving Sebastian's.

The EMT reached into his kit with a smile. "I think your friend Paul actually didn't need to help set you up. Looks like you're doing fine on your own."

The crowd burst into applause as Sebastian was helped to his feet by Endy and the EMT. When Paco rushed up, she let him take Sebastian's arm while she walked back to the stands. Climbing the first step, Endy saw Barbara Tennyson watching her. Endy ducked her head and tucked a strand of hair behind her ear.

But then Barbara gestured to Endy, patting the empty seat next to her. And as the music rang over Stadium Court, Barbara's and Endy's eyes locked and the two women smiled at each other.

Sebastian's knee was wrapped tightly and the back of his shirt and shorts were spotted with dirt from lying on the court. He limped toward his seat, trying not to put any pressure on his right leg. The EMT had iced and wrapped his knee and given him the Extra Strength Tylenol, all enough to allow him to stand.

But any weight or movement on his knee was excruciating. The EMT said if Sebastian continued to play, there was a possibility that he might do permanent damage to his knee.

The referee approached them, a timer clenched in her fist. She looked directly at Sebastian, now settled in a chair but still grimacing slightly. "You have about three minutes left on the medical time-out. Are you able to return to play?"

Paco, his chest puffed out, stepped in front of Sebastian and stared hard at the ref. "Give us some room, sister." He shooed her away. "My associate and I need to confer." Then he turned to Sebastian, looked him in the eye, and said, "Listen, loser"—his hands clutched at the front of his event T-shirt—"I need to tell you something."

Sebastian raised an eyebrow.

"Win or lose today, these have been the best months of my life, hanging with you."

Sebastian softened and he chuckled. "Paco, you're only ten. You have many more years—"

"Shut up, I'm talking." His big brown eyes filled. "I wanna thank you for believing in me . . . because no one else ever has."

Sebastian took a deep breath and pulled Paco into a hug.

"Jeez, get off me!" Paco struggled to get away, and Sebastian responded by laughing and squeezing Paco tighter.

"Okay, then let's go back out there and finish, win or lose."

Paco pulled away. "Seriously, Sebastian, if you're too messed up, we don't have to go back and play. You don't need to go out there for me."

"That's cool, Paco. But we *are* going back out." Sebastian resolutely nodded and pushed himself up to standing. "I'm finally on a court doing something for *me*."

"Time-in!" the referee announced. She rolled the ball to Paco. "Ten, ten, two."

Sebastian positioned himself in front of the baseline with his weight on his good leg. The newly wrapped bandage around his knee looked bright in the sunlight. He looked at Paco and nodded once.

Paco quickly dropped the ball, swiped at it, and sliced the serve. Unprepared, Brayden put his paddle out too late, and the ball landed on the court, twisting out to the right.

"Point!" called the ref. "Eleven, ten, two."

Sebastian hobbled to the other side of their court. Tension

was high, with the crowd on the edge of their seats, knowing that one point could decide the champions.

Taking a deep breath, Paco served to Joel, the ball landing deep.

Joel hit the ball to Paco, who returned the ball and then moved forward.

"Heads up, peewee." Joel smirked. And he lifted the ball in a lob over Paco's head.

Sebastian, anticipating Joel's shot, had hobbled closer to the middle, standing with all his weight on his good leg. With his long, muscular arms, he reached out and swatted at the ball, slamming it right into Joel's body. A gasp rang through the crowd.

Joel's paddle, which he had positioned close to his chest, deflected the ball, and it shot out, clearing the net, straight down the line, under Sebastian's still upraised arm to kiss the line, bouncing up and out.

But Paco, hidden behind Sebastian, darted across the court, a look of determination burning on his face. Gripping his paddle tightly, he dove toward the ball as it hung midair, and with the smallest of movements, delivered a smack that sent the ball sailing around the net post . . . landing it solidly in Joel and Brayden's court.

"Point. Game. And match," called out the pickleball ref. "Lopez, Hall. Twelve, ten."

The crowd jumped to their feet, erupting in screams and applause.

45

Sebastian gripped the back of Paco's collar, lifting up so Paco had to walk on his toes. Paco swiped his trophy behind him, through the air, trying to hit Sebastian.

"Congratulations, you two!" Steven Markowitz rushed up and clapped Sebastian on the back. He looked down at Paco with a kind smile. "Well done, son."

"Thanks." Paco blushed and looked at his feet. "Hey . . . I'm sorry I called you an *abuelo*."

"Paco, I'd be proud to be your *abuelo*," answered Steven. "Let's play sometime."

Paco gagged, then with a grimace replied, "I said that I was sorry, not that I was crazy." He pulled away from Sebastian's grasp and skipped down the pathway.

Endy approached them, laughing, her eyes crinkled at the corners. She stood on tiptoe and pecked Sebastian's cheek.

"That kid is wise beyond his years," she said, watching Paco wiggling his rear end to the music still playing through the grounds. He pumped his fist holding his trophy in the air to the beat of the music.

Steven moved to an empty table, flipped it over, and began folding in the legs. Around them, volunteers stacked chairs and emptied trash cans, breaking down the event. Empty cups, left-behind T-shirts and paddles, and other forgotten items littered the grounds.

From outside the tent, Valentina called out, her hand cupping her mouth, "Endy, we need to get going home. Paco is actually supposed to be grounded this week." Her mouth lifted in a half smile, and she shook her head. "Plus, we need to show off his trophy." She placed her hand on Paco's head, affectionately smoothing down his hair.

"Jeez, Mom," complained Paco, twisting out of her reach and moving down the pathway toward the parking lot. He knelt and picked up something from under a bougainvillea shrub, then turned and ran halfway back, as if he'd forgotten something.

Facing Sebastian and Endy, Paco yelled, "Hey, loser, you better tell her."

Sebastian nodded and gave him a thumbs-up.

"Tell me what?" Endy smiled, looking into Sebastian's eyes.

Sebastian wrapped her in his arms and placed his lips near her ear. "He wants me to tell you that—"

Clunk! A hard plastic ball flew through the air, hitting Sebastian solidly on the head. He reached up, rubbing near his ear.

And they watched Paco skip away, one hand hefting his trophy over his head, the other hand with his middle finger flipped high in the air.

"He wants me to tell you that . . ." Sebastian moved his lips near Endy's ear and pressed a kiss against her head. "I love you."

46

It still amazed Endy how quickly the weather in the desert could go from a beautiful, warm spring day with temperatures in the low eighties to a heatstroke-inducing, flaming-hot oven with temperatures in the low hundreds. She lifted her long hair off her sweaty neck and piled it on top of her head in a messy bun.

"Why are we headed to Costco?" she asked, turning in her seat with her eyes questioning.

Sebastian smiled mysteriously. "You'll see."

She angled the air vent at her face. "It's so hot. Can't we just go to your pool?"

"Maybe we aren't going to Costco. And we will get in the pool, but after this," he replied as he turned his car into the parking lot across the street. "Close your eyes."

"What—"

"Just close your eyes. And keep them closed."

Endy felt the car slow to a stop, and she kept her eyes shut. She heard Sebastian walk around the car and her door open.

His hand reached in for hers, and he pulled her out of her seat and then wrapped her in a tight hug.

"Don't open your eyes."

"I'm not! I'm not!" She frowned. "Can we just go? I'm so hot."

He turned her around and stood behind her, his hands on her shoulders. He leaned close to her ear, kissed the side of her head, then said, "Okay. You can open your eyes."

Endy's eyes opened to the sight of an enormous sign covering the front entrance of the empty building across the street from Costco.

PICKLE NATION
Indoor pickleball facility
Proud sponsor of Picklers Youth Pickleball League
OPENING SOON

Her mouth dropped open, and she screamed, "SHUT UP!"

She started jumping up and down with her arms raised over her head, pumping the air with her fists. "Oh my god, Sebastian! Is this yours?"

Sebastian grinned and nodded.

"*Yours!*" exclaimed Endy. She brought her hands to her cheeks in wonder. "And it's all pickleball? How many courts? Tell me everything!"

"Yes, and plenty. But see that row of windows?" He pointed to the upper portion of the building. "That's the most important part."

"What is that?"

"There's a live/work loft with a full kitchen, huge bathroom, bedrooms—"

"For who?"

"Well, for me . . ." Sebastian walked to his car, his limp barely noticeable. He opened the glove compartment and took out a teal-blue box tied with a white satin ribbon, which he then presented to Endy. "And I'd heard you were getting kicked out of your casita and needed someplace to live, so . . ."

Endy's eyebrows pulled together. She gently lifted the top off the small box, and nestled inside was a Tiffany key ring.

Sebastian dipped his head and pressed his lips to Endy's, tenderly kissing her.

"Welcome home, pickleball girl."

47

It stank. Even from all the way across the street, she could smell the harsh chemicals. A burned rubber odor carried over on the desert breeze. Draining the last sip of Rombauer from her wine glass, she quietly opened the metal gate from her patio and signaled to the dog. He got up from the warm pavers while she secured a leash to his leather collar, as HOA rules dictated.

They crossed onto the grass bordering the asphalt, now painted solid green and separated by two-inch-wide stripes. The reconverted single tennis court looked pristine once again.

Buttoning her cardigan against the evening chill, she gazed far out across the racquet club property to the area where eight new pickleball courts were being built in a previously unused grassy area. The construction crew had just poured the final topcoat, and the odor was still strong.

Barbara Tennyson pulled on Ollie's leash, and they walked to the bench overlooking the tennis court. Next to it stood a brand-new sign:

Whisper Hills Country Club
Junior Tennis Academy Court

She smiled and sat down on the bench. Barbara withdrew a cloth from her sweater pocket, turned to the back of the bench, and polished the attached plaque.

"Looks good, doesn't it?"

Barbara turned around as Sloane approached, her hand gesturing out to the tennis court.

"It certainly does," Barbara replied.

Barbara patted the seat next to her, and Sloane lowered herself into it. Barbara reached out and lightly grasped Sloane's hand. "Thank you, dear. For helping me make this happen."

"Mrs. Tennyson, it's an absolute honor to have your husband's court for the academy's exclusive use."

"It wasn't just Clive's court—"

"It wasn't officially, but in everyone's mind, it was," said Sloane. "And thank you for providing such a generous scholarship. Even though we had enough funding for the operations part of the academy, there will be many, many kids who can go on to achieve great things in tennis because of you and your family's gift."

They sat in companionable silence, an owl hooting above them from the nearby date palm tree.

"And what's next for you, dear?" asked Barbara, breaking the silence.

Sloane smiled. "Well, turns out that a position for assistant director of racquet sports just opened up here, so I took it. I'll hang around and run the tennis academy and try to keep the pickleballers honest." She chuckled, then sighed. "I wasn't ever the right girl for Sebastian . . . but Endy is."

Barbara nodded. "I've never seen him so happy. But I am sorry it didn't work out for you."

"Oh, don't worry about me," Sloane said with a smile. She opened her phone and turned it to Barbara. On the home screen was a photo of Sloane holding a tennis racquet and Wes clutching a pickleball paddle, the two of them with their arms around each other, beaming.

"Ah, another one of those mixed romances," replied Barbara. With that, she stood up from the bench. "I better get going. Ollie has to do his evening business, and we were headed to the dog park."

A loud cheer came from the pickleball courts, causing Ollie to startle. He pulled his leash from Barbara's hand, then darted away.

"Ollie, come back this instant," said Barbara, sharply. "Where did he go off to?"

From the safety under the bougainvillea bushes, they saw a black-and-white tail wagging, swishing back and forth. And then the dog backed out, turning toward his owner with something clenched in his teeth.

A bright green plastic pickleball.

He trotted back to Barbara and dropped the ball at her feet, his back end wiggling furiously.

"Ah . . ." Her lips lifted in a warm smile. "Who's a good boy?"

Acknowledgments

This year, like a lamb to the slaughter, I joined almost fifty million people worldwide hooked by the pickleball craze.

So it figures that I would have a blast learning to play the game and writing this book. I couldn't have done it without the support of some wonderful people: Alice and Nash. Van and Kathleen. And, of course, Jeremy.

My deepest thanks go to the following people: Tess Newton and the fantastic team at Greenleaf Book Group. Tom Agamenoni for beta reading. Angie Wingett for your invaluable opinions, beta reading, and always responding to my texts. Stacy Osugi for your graphics skills and annoying, but effective, forehand slice. Balinda Huang of bcomplex for your fabulous designs. Jeremy Sauter, for your creative brilliance, endless encouragement, and for footing all the bills.

And extra special appreciation goes to the OGs of our Mission Hills Wednesday Pickleball Group: Roser and Pete, Yvonne, Shawn, David, Tom and Ann, and most of all, John Wagner.

About the Author

REBECCA JASMINE was born and raised in a small town in northern Montana. Throughout her life, she has lived near the Golden Gate Bridge, the Sunset Strip, and the Panama Canal. Currently, she and her husband, Jeremy Sauter, live near the city of Palm Springs.

Rebecca worked for years in TV and movie advertising, was an official TSA Pre-check Enrollment Agent, and was on screen for seven seconds while being a background extra on *Yellowstone*, season 4, episode 1.

She laughs the most and screams the loudest when she's on a pickleball court. And whenever she travels, you can bet there's a paddle in her carry-on bag.

To receive updates, bonus content, and more, follow Rebecca on social media and sign up at www.rebeccajasmine.com. Her historical fiction novel, *The Copper King's Daughter*, is available on Amazon and in independent bookstores throughout Montana.

Join the Pickleball Girls Team

Go to my website, www.rebeccajasmine.com to:

- ★ Sign up and join the team of pickleball girls
- ★ Receive updates, bonus content, and exclusive sneak peeks as they become available
- ★ Shop for signed copies and Pickleball Girl and Whisper Hills Country Club merchandise
- ★ Get in touch to say hello and let me know about your best matches (on the court and off!)

Follow me on social media:

Instagram: @rebeccajasminewrites

Facebook: @Rebecca Jasmine - Author

And if you enjoyed reading *The Pickleball Girl Finds Her Match*, I'd really appreciate it if you would leave a review on Amazon or Goodreads.

WHISPER HILLS COUNTRY CLUB — Book 2

Psst!

Get ready for Whisper Hills Country Club's pickleball girl Maria Gutierrez's story in Book 2.

COMING OUT SOON!